GPAC
07/05

11-17-11

W9-CIM-243

Quincannon's Game

Other Five Star Titles
by Bill Pronzini:

All the Long Years
Burgade's Crossing
Scenarios: A "Nameless Detective" Casebook
Oddments: A Short Story Collection
More Oddments
Sleuths

Quincannon's Game

Western Stories

Bill Pronzini

Five Star • Waterville, Maine

Copyright © 2005 by the Pronzini-Muller Family Trust

"The Bughouse Caper" first appeared in *Sherlock Holmes: The Hidden Years* (St. Martin's Press, 2004). Copyright © 2004 by the Pronzini-Muller Family Trust.

"The Cloud Cracker" first appeared in *Louis L'Amour Western Magazine* (7/94). Copyright © 1994 by the Pronzini-Muller Family Trust.

"Medium Rare" first appeared in *Ellery Queen's Mystery Magazine* (9–10/98). Copyright © 1998 by the Pronzini-Muller Family Trust.

"Quincannon in Paradise" first appeared in *Ellery Queen's Mystery Magazine* (05). Copyright © 2005 by the Pronzini-Muller Family Trust.

All rights reserved.

This collection is a work of fiction. Names, characters, places and incidents are either the product of the author's imagination, or, if real, used fictitiously.

No part of this book may be reproduced or transmitted in any form or by any electronic or mechanical means, including photocopying, recording or by any information storage and retrieval system, without the express written permission of the publisher, except where permitted by law.

First Edition
First Printing: August 2005

Published in 2005 in conjunction with Golden West Literary Agency.

Set in 11 pt. Plantin by Elena Picard.

Printed in the United States on permanent paper.

Library of Congress Cataloging-in-Publication Data

Pronzini, Bill.
    Quincannon's game : western stories / by Bill Pronzini.—1st ed.
        p. cm.
    ISBN 1-59414-167-3 (hc : alk. paper)
    1. Western stories. I. Title
PS3566.R67Q554 2005
    813'.54—dc22   2005012058

S Western
Pronzini, Bill.
Quincannon's game : western
stories

Quincannon's Game

Table of Contents

The Bughouse Caper

I

The house at the westward edge of Russian Hill was a dormered and turreted pile of two stories and some dozen rooms, with a wraparound porch and a good deal of gingerbread trim. It was set well back from the street and well apart from its neighbors, given seclusion by shade trees, flowering shrubs, and marble statuary. A fine home, as befitted the likes of Samuel Truesdale, senior vice president of the San Francisco Maritime Bank. A home filled with all the playthings of the wealthy.

A home built to be burglarized.

Thirty feet inside the front gate, Quincannon shifted position in the deep shadow of a lilac bush. From this vantage point he had clear views of the house, the south side yard, and the street. He could see little of the rear of the property, where the bulk of a carriage barn loomed and a gated fence gave access to a carriageway that bisected the block, but this was of no consequence. His quarry might well come onto the property from that direction, but there was no rear entrance to the house and the method of preferred entry was by door, not first- or second-story windows; this meant he would have to come around to the side door or the front door, both of which were within clear sight.

No light showed anywhere on the grounds. Banker Truesdale and his wife, dressed to the nines, had left two hours earlier in a private carriage, and they had no live-in servants. The only light anywhere in the immediate vicinity came from a street lamp some fifty yards distant, a flickery glow that did not reach into the Truesdale yard. High cirro-stratus clouds made thin streaks across the sky, touching but not obscuring an early moon. The heavenly body was neither a sickle nor what the yeggs called a stool-pigeon moon, but a near half that dusted the darkness with enough pale shine to see by.

A night made for burglars and footpads. And detectives on the scent.

The combination of property and conditions was one of the reasons Quincannon had stationed himself here. The other was the list of names in the pocket of his Chesterfield, provided by Jackson Pollard of the Great Western Insurance Company—a list that was also in a housebreaker's pocket, obtained from an unscrupulous employee or through other nefarious means. Whatever the burglar's expense, it had rewarded him handsomely in two previous robberies. Tonight, if all went according to plan, it would be Carpenter and Quincannon, Professional Detective Services, who would reap the list's final reward.

Aye, and the sooner the better. A raw early May wind had sprung up, thick with the salt smell of the bay, and its chill penetrated the greatcoat, cheviot, gloves, neck scarf, and cap Quincannon wore. Noiselessly he stomped his feet and flexed his fingers to maintain circulation. His mind conjured up the image of steaming mugs of coffee and soup. Of a fire hot and crackling in his rooms on Leavenworth Street. Of the warmth of Sabina's lips on the distressingly few occasions he had tasted them, and the all too brief pressure of her splendid body against his, and the heat of his passion for her. . . .

Ah, no. None of that now. Attention to the matter at hand, detective business first and foremost. Why dwell on his one frustrating failure, when another of his professional triumphs was imminent? Easier to catch a crook than to melt a stubborn woman's resistance. Quincannon's Law.

A rattling and clopping on the cobbled street drew his attention. Moments later a hack, its side lamps casting narrow funnels of light, passed without slowing. When the sound of it faded, another sound took its place—music, faint and melodic. Someone playing the violin, and rather well, too. Quincannon listened for a time, decided what was being played were passages from Mendelssohn's *Lieder*. He was hardly an expert on classical music, or even much of an aficionado, but he had allowed Sabina to draw him to enough concerts to identify individual pieces. Among his strong suits as a detective were both a photographic memory and a well-tuned ear.

More time passed at a creep and crawl. The wind died down a lot, but he was so thoroughly chilled by then he scarcely noticed. Despite the heavy gloves and the constant flexing, his fingers felt stiff; much more time out here in the cold, and he might well have difficulty drawing his Navy Colt if such became necessary.

Blast this blasted housebreaker, whoever he was! He was bound to come after the spoils tonight; Quincannon was sure of it, and his instincts seldom led him astray. So what was the scruff waiting for? It must be after nine by now. Wherever banker Truesdale and his missus had gone for the evening, chances were they would return by eleven. This being Thursday, Truesdale's presence would surely be required tomorrow morning at his bank.

Quincannon speculated once more on the identity of his quarry. There were dozens of house burglars in San Francisco and environs, but the cleverness of method and skill of entry in this case narrowed the field to a few professionals. Of those known to him, the likeliest candidates were the Sanctimonious Kid and Dodger Brown. Both were known to be in the Bay area at present, but neither had done anything else to attract attention, such as immediately fencing stolen jewelry and other valuables. And if the man responsible was a newcomer, he was of the same professional stripe. In any case, the swag had surely been planted for the nonce, to be disposed of after the thief had gone through most or all of the five names on the target list.

Or so the yegg would believe. Quincannon relished the prospect of convincing him otherwise, almost as much as he relished the thought of collecting the fat fee from Great Western Insurance.

The violin music had ceased; the night was hushed again. He flexed and stomped and shifted and shivered, his mood growing darker by the minute. If the burglar gave any trouble, he would rue the effort. Quincannon prided himself as a man of guile and razor-sharp wits, but he was also a brawny man of Pennsylvania Scots stock and not averse to a bit of thumping and skull dragging if the situation warranted.

Another vehicle, a small carriage this time, clattered past. A figure appeared on the sidewalk, and Quincannon tensed expectantly—but it was only a citizen walking his dog, and soon gone. Hell and damn! If by some fluke he *was* wrong about the place and time of the next burglary, and he was forced to spend another evening courting pneumonia or worse, he would demand a bonus from Jackson Pollard. And if he didn't get it, he would damned well pad the expense account whether Sabina approved or not.

But he wasn't wrong. That became evident in the next

few seconds, when he turned his gaze from the street to the inner yard and house.

Someone was moving over there, not fifty yards from where Quincannon was hidden.

His senses all sharpened at once; he stood immobile, peering through the lilac's branches. The movement came again, a shadow drifting among stationary shadows, at an angle from the rear of the property toward the side porch. Once the shape reached the steps and started up, it was briefly silhouetted—a man in dark clothing and a low-pulled cap. Then it merged with the deeper black on the porch. Several seconds passed. Then there was a brief stab of light—the beam from a dark lantern such as the one in Quincannon's pocket—followed by the faintest of scraping sounds as the intruder worked with his tools.

Once again stillness closed down. He was inside now. Quincannon stayed where he was, marking time. No light showed behind the dark windows. The professional burglar worked mainly by feel and instinct, using his lantern sparingly and shielding the beam when he did.

When Quincannon judged ten minutes had passed, he left his hiding place and cat-footed through shadows until he was parallel with the side porch stairs. He paused to listen, heard nothing from the house, and crossed quickly, bent low, to a tall rhododendron planted alongside the steps. Here he hunkered down on one knee to wait.

The wait might be another ten minutes; it might be a half hour or more. No matter. Now that the crime was in progress, he no longer minded the cold night, the dampness of the earth where he knelt. Even if there were a locked safe, no burglar would leave premises such as these without spoils of some sort. Art objects, silverware, anything of value that could be carried off and subsequently sold to pawnbrokers or one of the many fences that operated in the city. Whatever this lad emerged with, it would be enough for Quincannon to yaffle him. Whether he turned his man over to the city police immediately or not depended on the scruff's willingness to reveal the whereabouts of the swag from his previous jobs. Stashing and rough-housing a prisoner for information was unethical, if not illegal, but Quincannon felt righteously that in the pursuit of justice, not to mention a fat fee, the end justified the means.

His wait lasted less than thirty minutes. The creaking of a floorboard pricked up his ears, creased his freebooter's beard with a smile of anticipation. Another creak, the faintest squeak of a door hinge, a footfall on the porch. Now descending the steps, into Quincannon's view—short, slender, but turned out of profile so that his face was obscured. He paused on the bottom step, and in that moment Quincannon levered up and put the grab on him.

He was much the larger man, and there should have been no trouble in the catch. But just before his arms closed around the wiry body, the yegg heard or sensed danger and reacted not by trying to run or turning to fight, but by dropping suddenly into a crouch. Quincannon's arms slid up and off as if greased, pitching him off balance. The scruff bounced upright, swung around, blew the stench of sour wine into Quincannon's face at the same time he fetched him a stabbing kick in the shin. Quincannon let out a howl, staggered, and nearly fell. By the time he caught himself, his quarry was on the run.

He gave chase on the blind, cursing inventively and sulphurously, hobbling for the first several steps until the pain from the kick ebbed. The burglar had twenty yards on him by then, zigzagging toward the bordering yew trees, then back away from them in the direction of the carriage barn. In the moonshine he made a fine, clear target, but Quincannon did not draw his Navy Colt. Ever since the long-ago episode in Virginia City, Nevada, when one of his stray bullets fired during a battle with counterfeiters had claimed an innocent woman's life and led him into a guilt-ridden two-year bout with demon rum, he had vowed to use his weapon only if his life was in mortal danger. He had never broken that vow. Nor touched a drop of liquor since entering into his partnership with Sabina.

Before reaching the barn, his man cut away at another angle and plowed through a gate into the carriageway beyond. Quincannon lost sight of him for a few seconds, spied him again as he reached the gate and barreled through it. A race down the alley? No. The scruff was nimble as well as slippery; he threw a look over his shoulder, saw Quincannon in close pursuit, suddenly veered sideways and flung himself up and over a six-foot board fence into one of the neighboring yards.

In six long strides Quincannon was at the fence. He caught the top boards, hoisted himself up to chin level. Some fifty yards distant was the backside of a stately home, two windows and a pair of French doors ablaze with electric light; the outward spill combined with pale moonshine to limn a jungly garden, a path leading through its profusion of plants and trees to a gazebo on the left. He had a brief glimpse of a dark shape plunging into shrubbery near the gazebo.

Quincannon scrambled up the rough boards, rolled his body over the top. And had the misfortune to land awkwardly on his sore leg, which gave way and toppled him, skidding to his knees in damp grass. He growled an oath under his breath, lumbered to his feet, and stood listening. Leaves rustled and branches snapped—moving away from the gazebo now, toward the house.

The path was of crushed shell that gleamed with a faint, ghostly radiance; he drifted along parallel to it, keeping to the grass to cushion his footfalls. Gnarled cypress and tall thorny pyracantha bushes partially obscured the house, the shadows under and around them as black as India ink. He paused to listen again. No more sounds of movement. He started forward, eased around one of the cypress trees.

The man who came up behind him did so with such silent stealth that he had no inkling of the other's presence until a hard object poked into and stiffened his spine and a forceful voice said: "Stand fast, if you value your life. There's a good fellow."

Quincannon stood fast.

II

The one who had the drop on him was not the man he'd been chasing. The calm, cultured, and British-accented voice, and the almost casual choice of words, told him that. He said, stifling his anger and frustration: "I'm not a prowler."

"What are you, then?"

"A detective on the trail of a thief. I chased him into this yard."

"Indeed?" His captor sounded interested, if not convinced. "What manner of thief?"

"A blasted housebreaker. He broke into the Truesdale home."

"Did he, now. Mister Truesdale, the banker?"

"That's right. Your neighbor across the carriageway."

"A mistaken assumption. This is not my home, and I've

only just met Mister Truesdale tonight."

"Then who are you?"

"All in good time. This is hardly a proper place for introductions."

"Introductions be damned," Quincannon growled. "While we stand here gabbing, the thief is getting away."

"Has already gotten away, I should think. Perhaps. . . ."

"Perhaps?"

"If you're who you say you are and not a thief yourself." The hard object prodded his backbone. "Move along to the house and we'll have the straight of things in no time."

"Bah," Quincannon said, but he moved along.

There was a flagstone terrace across the rear of the house, and, when they reached it, he could see people in evening clothes moving around a well-lighted parlor. His captor took him to a pair of French doors, ordered him to step inside. Activity in the room halted when they entered. Six pairs of eyes, three male and three female, stared at him and the man behind him. One of the couples, both plump and middle-aged, was Samuel Truesdale and his wife. The others were strangers.

The parlor was large, handsomely furnished, dominated by a massive grand piano. On the piano bench lay a well-used violin and bow—the source of the passages from Mendelssohn he had heard earlier, no doubt. A wood fire blazed on the hearth. A combination of the fire and steam heat made the room too warm, stuffy. Quincannon's benumbed cheeks began to tingle almost immediately.

The first to break the frozen tableau was a round-faced gent with Lincolnesque whiskers and ears as large as the handles on a pickle jar. He stepped forward and demanded of the Englishman: "Where did this man come from? Who is he?"

17

"On my stroll in the garden I spied him climbing the fence and apprehended him. He claims to be a detective on the trail of a panny-man. Housebreaker, that is."

"I don't claim to be a detective," Quincannon said sourly, "I *am* a detective. Quincannon's the name, John Quincannon."

"Doctor Caleb Axminster," the whiskered gent said. "What's this about a housebreaker?"

The exchange drew the others closer in a tight little group. It also brought the owner of the cultured English voice out to where Quincannon could see him for the first time. He wasn't such-a-much. Tall, excessively lean, with a thin, hawk-like nose and a prominent chin. In one hand he carried a blackthorn walking stick, held midway along the shaft. Quincannon scowled. It must have been the stick, not a pistol that had poked his spine and allowed the burglar to escape.

"I'll ask you again," Dr. Axminster said. "What's this about a housebreaker?"

"I chased him here from a neighbor's property." Quincannon switched his gaze to the plump banker. He was not a man to mince words, even at the best of times. And this was not the best of times. "Your home, Mister Truesdale," he said bluntly.

Mrs. Truesdale and the other women gasped. Her husband's face lost its healthy color. "Mine? Good Lord, man, do you mean to say we've been robbed?"

"Unfortunately, yes. Do you keep your valuables in a safe?"

"My wife's jewelry and several stock certificates, yes."

"Cash?"

"In my desk . . . a hundred dollars or so in greenbacks. . . ." Truesdale shook his head; he seemed dazed. "You were there?"

"I was. Waiting outside."

"Waiting? I don't understand."

"To catch the burglar in the act."

"But how did you know . . . ?"

"Detective work, suffice it to say."

The fifth man in the room had been silent to this point. He was somewhat younger than the others, forty or so, dark-eyed, clean-shaven; his most prominent feature was a misshapen knob of red-veined flesh, like a partially collapsed balloon, that seemed to hang between his eyes and a thin-lipped mouth. He aimed a brandy snifter at Quincannon and said challengingly: "If you were set up to catch the housebreaker, why didn't you? What happened?"

"An unforeseen occurrence." Quincannon glared sideways at his gaunt captor. "I would have chased him down if this man hadn't accosted me."

"Accosted?" The Englishman arched an eyebrow. "Dear me, hardly that. I had no way of knowing you weren't a prowler."

Mrs. Truesdale was tugging at her husband's arm. "Samuel, hadn't we best return home and find out what was stolen?"

"Yes, yes, immediately."

"Margaret," Axminster said to one of the other women, a slender graying brunette with patrician features, "find James and have him drive the Truesdales."

The woman nodded and left the parlor with the banker and his wife in tow.

The doctor said then—"This is most distressing."—but he didn't sound distressed. He sounded excited, as if he found the situation stimulating. He produced a paper sack from his pocket, popped a hoarhound drop into his mouth.

"But right up your alley, eh, Mister Holmes?"

The Englishmen bowed.

"And yours, Andrew. Eh? The law and all that."

"Hardly," the dark-eyed man said. "You know I handle civil, not criminal, cases. Why don't you introduce us, Caleb? Unless Quincannon already knows who I am, too."

Quincannon decided he didn't particularly like the fellow. Or Axminster, for that matter. Or the blasted Englishman. In fact, he did not like anybody tonight, not even himself very much.

"Certainly," the doctor said. "This is Andrew Costain, Mister Quincannon, and his wife Penelope. And this most distinguished gentleman. . . ."

"Costain?" Quincannon interrupted. "Offices on Geary Street, residence near South Park?"

"By God," Costain said, "he *does* know me. But if we've met, I don't remember the time or place. In court, was it?"

"We haven't met anywhere. Your name happens to be on the list."

"List?" Penelope Costain said. She was a slender, gray-eyed, brown-curled woman some years younger than her husband—handsome enough, although she appeared too aloof and wore too much rouge and powder for Quincannon's taste. "What list?"

"Of potential burglary victims, all of whom own valuables insured by the Great Western Insurance Company."

"So that's it," Costain said. "Truesdale's name is also on that list, I suppose. That's what brought you to his home tonight."

"Among other things," Quincannon admitted.

Axminster sucked the hoarhound drop, his brow screwed up in thought. "Quincannon, John Quincannon . . . why, of course! I knew I'd heard the name before. Carpenter and

Quincannon, Professional Detective Services. Yes, and your partner is a woman. Sabina Carpenter."

"A woman," the Englishman said. "How curious."

Quincannon skewered him with a sharp eye. "What's curious about it? Both she and her late husband were valued operatives attached to the Pinkerton Agency's Denver office."

"Upon my soul. In England, you know, it would be extraordinary for a woman to assume the profession of consulting detective, the more so to be taken in as a partner in a private inquiry agency."

"She wasn't taken in, as you put it. Our partnership was by mutual arrangement."

"Ah."

"What do you know of private detectives, in England or anywhere?"

"He knows a great deal, as a matter of fact," Axminster said with relish. He asked the Englishman: "You have no objection if I reveal your identity to a colleague?"

"None, inasmuch as you have already revealed it to your guests."

The doctor beamed. He said as if presenting a member of the British royalty: "My honored house guest, courtesy of a mutual acquaintance in the south of France, is none other than Mister Sherlock Holmes of Two Twenty-One-B Baker Street, London."

The Englishman bowed. "At your service."

"I've already had a sampling of your service," Quincannon said aggrievedly. "I prefer my own."

"Nous verrons."

"Holmes, is it? I'm not familiar with the name."

"Surely you've heard it," Axminster said. "Not only has Mister Holmes solved many baffling cases in England and

21

Europe, but his apparent death at the hands of his arch enemy, Professor Moriarity, was widely reported three years ago."

"I seldom read sensational news."

"Officially," Holmes said, "I am still dead, having been dispatched at Reichenbach Falls in Switzerland. For private reasons I've chosen to let this misapprehension stand, until recently confiding in no one but my brother Mycroft. Not even my good friend Doctor Watson knows I'm still alive."

"If he's such a good friend, why haven't you told him?"

Holmes produced an enigmatic smile and made no reply.

Axminster said: "Doctor John H. Watson is Mister Holmes's biographer as well as his friend. The doctor has chronicled many of his cases."

"Yes?"

" 'A Study in Scarlet', the 'Red-Headed League', the 'Sign of the Four', the horror at Baskerville Hall, the adventure of the six orange pips. . . ."

"Five," Holmes said.

"Eh? Oh, yes, five orange pips."

Quincannon said: "I've never heard of any of them." The stuffily overheated room was making him sweat. He stripped off his gloves, unbuttoned his Chesterfield, and swept the tails back. At the same time he essayed a closer look at the Englishman, which led him somewhat to revise his earlier estimate. The fellow might be gaunt, almost cadaverous in his evening clothes, but his jaw and hawk-like nose bespoke intensity and determination, and his eyes were sharp, piercing, alive with a keen intelligence. It would be a mistake to dismiss him too lightly.

Holmes said with a gleam of interest: "I daresay you've had your own share of successes, Quincannon."

"More than I can count."

"Oh, yes, Mister Quincannon is well known locally," the doctor said. "Several of his investigations involving seemingly impossible crimes have gained notoriety. If I remember correctly, there was the rainmaker shot to death in a locked room, the strange disappearance on board the Desert Limited, the rather amazing murder of a bogus medium. . . ."

Holmes leaned forward. "I would be most interested to know what methods you and your partner employ."

"Methods?"

"In solving your cases. Aside from the use of weapons, fisticuffs, and such surveillance techniques as you employed tonight."

"What happened tonight was not my fault," Quincannon said testily. "As to our methods . . . those you mentioned, plus guile, wit, attention to detail, and deduction."

"Capital! My methods are likewise based on observation, in particular the observation of trifles, and on deductive reasoning . . . the construction of a series of inferences, each dependent upon its predecessor. An exact knowledge of all facets of crime and its history is invaluable as well, as I'm sure you know."

Bumptious gent! Quincannon managed not to sneer.

"For instance," Holmes said, smiling, "I should say that you are unmarried, smoke a well-seasoned briar, prefer cable twist Virginia tobacco, spent part of today in a tonsorial parlor and another part engaged in a game of straight pool, dined on chicken croquettes before proceeding to the Truesdale property, waited for your burglar in a shrub of *syringa persica,* and . . . oh, yes, under your rather tough exterior, I perceive that you are well-read and rather sensitive and sentimental."

Quincannon gaped at him. "How the devil can you know all that?"

"There is a loose button and loose thread on your vest, and your shirt collar is slightly frayed . . . telltale indications of our shared state of bachelorhood. When I stood close behind you in the garden, I detected the scent of your tobacco . . . and, once in here, I noted a small spot of ash on the sleeve of your coat which confirmed the mixture and the fact that it was smoked in a well-aged briar. It happens, you see, that I once wrote a little monograph on the ashes of one hundred forty different types of cigar, pipe, and cigarette tobacco and am considered an authority on the subject. Your beard has been recently and neatly trimmed, as has your hair which retains a faint scent of bay rum . . . hence your visit to the tonsorial parlor. Under the nail of your left thumb is dust of the type of chalk commonly used on the lips of pool cues, and while billiards is often played in America, straight pool has a larger following and strikes me as more to your taste. On the handkerchief you used a moment ago to mop your forehead is a small, fresh stain the color and texture of which identifies it to the trained eye as having come from a dish of chicken croquettes. Another scent which clings faintly to your coat is that of *syringa persica,* or Persian lilac, indicating that you have recently spent time in close proximity to such a flowering shrub, and inasmuch as there are no lilac bushes in Doctor Axminster's garden, Mister Truesdale's property is the obvious deduction. I perceive that you are well read from the slim volume of poetry tucked into the pocket of your frock coat, and that you are both sensitive and sentimental from the identity of the volume's author. Emily Dickinson's poems, I am given to understand, are famous for those very qualities."

There was a moment of silence. Quincannon, for once in

his life, was at loss for words.

Axminster clapped his hands and exclaimed delightedly: "Amazing!"

"Elementary," Holmes said.

Penelope Costain yawned. "Mister Holmes has been regaling us with his powers of observation and deduction all evening. Frankly I found his prowess with the violin of greater amusement."

Her husband was likewise unimpressed. He had refilled his glass from a sideboard nearby and now emptied it again in a swallow; his face was flushed, his eyes slightly glazed. "Mental gymnastics are all well and good," he said with some asperity, "but we've stayed well away from the issue here. Which is that my name, Penelope's and mine, is on Quincannon's list of potential robbery victims."

"I wouldn't be concerned, Andrew," Axminster said. "After tonight's escapade, that fellow wouldn't dare attempt another burglary."

Quincannon said: "True enough. Particularly if he suspects that I know his identity."

"You recognized him?"

"After a fashion."

"Then why don't you go find him and have him arrested?" Costain demanded.

"All in good time. I guarantee he won't do any more breaking and entering this night."

Mrs. Costain asked: "Did you also guarantee catching him red-handed at the Truesdale's home?"

Quincannon had had enough of this company; much more of it and he might well say something even he would regret. He made a small show of consulting his stem-winder. "If you'll all excuse me," he said then, "I'll be on my way."

"To request police assistance?"

"To determine the extent of the Truesdales' loss."

Dr. Axminster showed him to the front door. The Costains remained in the parlor, and Sherlock Holmes tagged along. At the front door the Englishman said: "I must say, Quincannon, I regret my intervention in the garden, well-intentioned though it was, but I must say I found the interlude stimulating. It isn't often I have the pleasure of meeting a distinguished colleague while a game's afoot."

Quincannon reluctantly accepted the Englishman's proffered hand, clasped the doctor's just as briefly, and took his leave. Nurturing as he went the dark thought of a game involving *his* foot that he'd admire to play with Mr. Sherlock Holmes.

III

Sabina was already at her desk when Quincannon arrived at the Market Street offices of Carpenter and Quincannon, Professional Detective Services, the following morning. Poring over their financial ledger and bank records—a task he gladly left to her, since he had no head for figures. Other than hers, that was.

She was not a beautiful woman, but at thirty-one she possessed a healthy and mature comeliness that melted his hard Scot's heart. There was strength in her high-cheekboned face, intelligence in eyes the color of dark blue velvet. Her seal-black hair, layered high and fastened with a jeweled comb, glistened with bluish highlights in the pale sunlight slanting in through the windows at her back. And her figure . . . ah, her figure. Fine, slim, delicately rounded and curved in a lacy white shirtwaist and a Balmoral skirt.

Many men found her attractive, to be sure, and, as a young widow, fair game. If any had been allowed inside her Russian Hill flat, he wasn't aware of it; she was a strict guardian of her private life. He knew she was fond of him, yet she continually spurned his advances. This not only frustrated him, but left him in a state of constant apprehension. The very thought that she might accept a proposal of either dalliance or marriage from anyone but John Quincannon was maddening.

She had a sharp eye for his moods. The first thing she said was: "Well, John, from the look of you, all failed to go as planned at the Truesdale home."

"A fair assessment." Quincannon shed his Chesterfield and derby, hung them on the clothes tree, and retreated to his desk. He loaded his briar with shaved cable twist from his pouch, fired the tobacco with a lucifer. As he puffed, the skin along his brow furrowed. "Unique scent," he muttered. "Monograph on a hundred and forty different types of tobacco ash. *Faugh!*"

"What's that you're grumbling about?"

"Gent I encountered last night, blast the luck. Damned infuriating Englishman. Not only did he cost me the burglar's capture, he did his level best to make a fool of me with a bagful of parlor tricks."

Sabina raised an eyebrow. "How did that come about? Exactly what happened last night, John?"

He told her in some detail, most of it accurate to a fault. When he was done, she said: "So this English fellow is a detective, too. His name is Holmes, you said?"

"Sherlock Holmes." Quincannon puffed furiously on his briar. "Sherlock! What kind of name is that?"

"A most respected one, I do believe."

"Eh?"

"I've heard mention of the exploits of Mister Sherlock Holmes," Sabina said. "He has a sterling reputation. A fascinating man, by all accounts."

"Not by mine. Fascinating isn't the word I would use to describe him."

"Well, you didn't make his acquaintance under the best of circumstances."

"It wouldn't have mattered where I made his acquaintance. If he were handing me a bag of gold sovereigns, I would still find him an arrogant show-off."

"Arrogance is the trademark of a successful detective, you know."

"Yes? I've blessed little of it in me."

Sabina laughed. "Come now, John. You mean to say you weren't even a little impressed by Mister Holmes's powers of observation and deduction? Or his record of successes in England and Europe?"

"Not a bit's worth," Quincannon lied. "He may be a competent fly cop in his own bailiwick, but his genius is suspect. A mentalist in a collar-and-elbow variety show at the Bella Union could perform the same tricks. World's greatest detective? Bah!"

"Poor John. You did have rather a difficult evening, didn't you?"

"Difficult, yes, but not wholly unproductive."

"You're convinced Dodger Brown is the man we're after?"

"Reasonably. When he slipped loose and swung around to kick me. . . ."

"Kick you? I thought you said you slipped on the wet grass."

"Yes, yes," Quincannon lied again, "but how he got away is of no consequence. The important fact is that he was of the right size and that he reeked of cheap wine. Dodger Brown's weakness is foot juice."

"Yes, I remember."

He rummaged among the papers on his desk. "Where's that dossier on the Dodger?"

"Your left hand is resting on it."

So it was. He caught up the paper, scanned through it to refresh his memory. Dodger Brown, christened Hezekiah Gabriel Brown, had been born in Stockton twenty-nine years ago. Orphaned at an early age, ran away at thirteen, fell in with a bunch of rail-riding yeggs, and been immersed in criminal activity ever since, exclusively house burglary in recent years. Arrested numerous times and put on the small book—held as a suspicious character—by police in San Francisco, Oakland, and other cities. Served two terms in prison, the last at Folsom for stealing a pile of green-and-greasy from a miserly East Bay politician. Known traits: close-mouthed, willing to suffer all manner of abuse rather than give up spoils or acquaintances. Known confidantes: none. Known habits: frequenter of Oriental parlor houses, cheap-jack gambling halls, and Barbary Coast wine dumps, in particular Jack Foyles' on Kearney. Current whereabouts: unknown. Damn little information, but perhaps just enough.

When he lowered the dossier, Sabina said: "If he recognized you last night, he may have already unplanted his loot and gone on the lammas."

"I don't think so. It was too dark for him to see my face any more clearly than I saw his. For all he knows, I might have been Truesdale home early, or a neighbor who spotted him skulking. A greedy lad like the Dodger isn't likely to cut and run when he's flush and onto a string of profitable marks."

"After such a narrow escape, would he be bold enough to try burgling another home on the insurance company's list?"

"Possibly. He's none too bright, foolish, and as arrogant in his fashion as that Holmes gent. It was a bughouse caper that landed him in Folsom prison two years ago. He's not above another, I'll wager."

"What will you do if you find him?"

"There's little profit in bracing him. I'll locate the place he's holed up, search his rooms for evidence or word of which fence man he's approached."

"You intend to avoid reporting to Jackson Pollard first, I trust?"

Quincannon nodded grimly. Not only cash had been stolen from the Truesdale home but also a valuable necklace the banker's wife had neglected to lock away in their safe. Last night's urgings to the banker to wait before filing an insurance claim had fallen on deaf ears; Truesdale intended to do so immediately. Pollard would not take kindly to either the claim or word of Quincannon's failure to apprehend the thief.

"If Pollard should stop by here," he said, "tell him Mister Sherlock Holmes is responsible for the night's fiasco and I'm busy working to atone for his mistake."

"That's hardly tactful, John."

"Tact be damned. A fact is a fact."

He was re-donning his coat when a knock sounded on the entrance door and a frog-faced youth wearing a cap and baggy trousers entered. The cap sported a sewn decal proclaiming his employer to be Citywide Messenger Service. The youth confirmed it in a scratchy voice and stated that he had a message for Mr. John Quincannon, Esquire.

"I'll have it." Quincannon accepted the envelope, signed

for it, tore it open. The youth, looking hopeful, remained standing there. "Well? You've done your duty, lad. Off with you!" The command, accompanied by a fiercely menacing scowl and a step forward, sent the messenger scuttling hurriedly through the door.

Sabina said: "You might have slipped him a nickel, John."

"I did him a good turn by not tipping him. He'd only have spent it on profligate pleasures."

He finished opening the envelope, removed a sheet of bond paper that bore the letterhead and signature of Andrew Costain, Attorney-at-Law. The curt message, written in a rather ornate hand, read:

> I should like to discuss a business matter with you. If you will call on me today at my offices, at your convenience, I am sure you will find it to your professional and financial advantage.

He read the message aloud to Sabina. She said: "Regarding the burglaries, do you suppose?"

"Likely. He's the worry-wart type."

"You'll call on him, then, of course."

Quincannon glanced again at the paper, at the mellifluous phrase, **financial advantage**. "Of course," he said.

IV

Jack Foyles' was a shade less disreputable than most wine dumps, if only because it was equipped with a small lunch counter where its habitués could supplement their liquid sustenance with stale bread and a bowl of stew made from discarded vegetables, meat trimmings, bones, and chunks of tallow. Otherwise, there was little to distinguish it from its brethren. Barrels of "foot juice" and "red ink" behind a long bar, rows of rickety tables in three separate rooms lined with men and a few women of all types, ages, and backgrounds, a large open-floored area to accommodate those who had drunk themselves into a stupor. Porters who were themselves winos served the cheap and deadly drink in vessels supplied by junkmen—beer glasses, steins, pewter mugs, cracked soup bowls, tin cans. There was much loud talk, but never any laughter. Foyles' customers had long ago lost their capacity for mirth.

No one paid Quincannon the slightest attention as he moved slowly through the crowded rooms. Slurred voices rolled surf-like against his ears, identifying the speakers as lawyers, sailors, poets, draymen, road bums, scholars, factory workers, petty criminals. There were no class distinctions here, or seldom any trouble; they were all united by failure, bitterness, disillusionment, old age, disease, and unquenchable thirst for the grape. If there was anything positive to be said of wine dumps, it was that they were havens of democracy. Most customers would be here every day, or as often as they could panhandle or steal enough money to pay for their allotment of slow death, but a few, not yet far gone, were less frequent visitors—binge drinkers and slummers who found the atmosphere and the company to their liking. Many of these were crooks of one stripe or another, Dodger Brown among them.

But there was no sign of the Dodger today. Quincannon questioned two of the porters; one knew him and reported that he hadn't been to Foyles' in more than a week. Did the porter know where Dodger Brown might be found? The porter did not.

Quincannon left Foyles' and made his way into the heart of the Barbary Coast. During the daylight hours, the devil's playground seemed quiet, almost tame—a deceit if ever there was one. Less than a third as many predators and their prey prowled the ulcerous streets as could be found here after sundown; most gamblers, pickpockets, swindlers, shanghaiers, footpads, and roaming prostitutes were creatures of the night, and it was the dark hours when the preponderance of their prey succumbed to the gaudy lure of sin and wickedness. Some of the more notorious gambling dens and parlor houses were open for business, as were the scruffier cribs and deadfalls, but they were thinly populated at this hour. And mostly absent was the nighttime babel of pianos, hurdy-gurdies, drunken laughter, the cries of shills and barkers, and the shouts and screams of victims. Quincannon was anything but a prude, having done his fair share of carousing during his drinking days, but the Coast had never attracted him. He preferred to satisfy his vices in private.

Near Broadway there was a section of run-down hotels and lodging houses. He entered one of the latter and had words with the desk clerk, a runty chap named Galway—one of several of the Coast's underclass who were willing to sell information for cash or favors. Galway admitted to having seen Dodger Brown a time or two in recent weeks, and thought he might be residing at Foghorn Annie's, one of the seamen's boarding houses on the waterfront.

Quincannon found a hack on Montgomery—he always rode in hansoms when a client was paying expenses—and was shortly delivered to the Embarcadero. The trip turned out to be wasted time. Scruffs were known to seek shelter among seafaring men now and then, by pretending to be former sailors themselves or by paying extra for the protective coloration. Dodger Brown was known at Foghorn Annie's, but not a current resident. Visits to two other houses in the area produced neither the Dodger nor a clue to his whereabouts.

Hunger prodded Quincannon into a waterfront eatery, where he made short work of half a dozen oysters on the half shell and a bowl of fish stew. Another hack returned him to the Barbary Coast. He canvassed two other wine dumps, half a dozen gambling halls, and two parlor houses that featured "Asian specialties" without so much as a whisper of his quarry. The Dodger may have been a foolish dolt, but he was also sly enough to curtail his baser appetites and avoid his habitual haunts for the time being.

Enough of roaming the Coast, Quincannon decided. The time had come to call on Ezra Bluefield again. He had already approached the man once this week, just two days ago, seeking information on the house burglaries and possible fencing of the loot, and Bluefield grew testy when he was asked for too many favors. But if there was one lad in the devil's playground who could find out where Dodger Brown was holed up, it was Bluefield.

Quincannon walked to Terrific Street, as Pacific Avenue was called, turned into an alley, and entered a scabrous building in mid-block. A sign in blood-red letters above the entrance proclaimed the establishment to be the **Scarlet Lady Saloon**. A smaller sign beneath it read: **Ezra Bluefield, Prop**.

At one time the Scarlet Lady had been an infamous crimping joint, where seamen were fed drinks laced with laudanum and chloral hydrate and then carted off by shanghaiers and sold to unscrupulous shipmasters in need of crews. The Sailor's Union of the Pacific had ended the practice and forced the saloon's closure, but only until

Bluefield had promised to end his association with the shanghaiers and backed up the promise with generous bribes to city officials. The Scarlet Lady was now an "honest" deadfall in which percentage girls, bunco ploys, and rigged games of chance were used to separate seamen and other patrons from their money.

As usual, Bluefield was in his office at the rear. He was an ex-miner who had had his fill of the rough-and-tumble life in various Western gold fields and vowed to give up his own rowdy ways when he moved to San Francisco and opened the Scarlet Lady. He had taken no active part in the crimping activities, and was known to remain behind his locked office door when brawls broke out, as they often did; the team of bouncers he employed were charged with stifling trouble and keeping what passed for peace. It was his stated intention to one day own a better class of saloon in a better neighborhood, and as a result he cultivated the company and good will of respectable citizens. Quincannon was one of them, largely because he had once prevented a rival saloon owner from puncturing Bluefield's hide with a bullet.

Bluefield was drinking beer and counting profits, two of his favorite activities, and seemed not to mind being visited again so soon. "I've nothing for you yet, John, my lad," he said. "You know I'll send word when I do."

"I'm the one with news today," Quincannon said. "The housebreaker I'm after is Dodger Brown."

"The Dodger, is it? Well, I'm not surprised. How did you tumble?"

"I came within a hair of nabbing him in the act last night. He escaped through no fault of mine."

"So he knows you're onto him?"

"I don't believe he does, as dark as it was."

"He'll still be in the vicinity then, you're thinking,"

35

Bluefield said. He raised his mug of lager with one thick finger, drank, licked foam off his mustached upper lip. The mustache was an impressive coal-black handlebar, its ends waxed to rapier points, of which he was inordinately proud. "And mayhap old Ezra can find out where he's hanging his hat."

"You'll make me a happy man if it can be done quickly."

"I'll put out the word. A favor in return, John?"

"Name it."

"There's a saloon and restaurant just up for sale in the Uptown Tenderloin. The Redemption, on Ellis Street."

"I know it. A respected establishment."

"I'm looking to buy it," Bluefield said. "It's past time I put this hellhole up for sale and leave the Coast for good. There'll never be a place better suited or better named for the likes of me to die a respectable citizen. I have the money, I've made overtures, but the owners aren't convinced my intentions are honorable. They're afraid I have plans to turn the Redemption into a fancy copy of the Scarlet Lady."

"And you've no such plans."

"None, lad, I swear it."

"Is it a letter of reference you're after, then?"

"Yes. Your name carries weight in this city."

"You'll have it tomorrow, by messenger."

Bluefield lumbered to his feet and thumped Quincannon's back with a meaty paw. "You won't regret it, John. You and your lady partner will never pay for a meal at Ezra Bluefield's Redemption."

Quincannon had never turned down a free meal in his life, and never would. "I'll settle for word of Dodger Brown's whereabouts," he lied.

"Within twenty-four hours," Bluefield said, "and that's a

36

bloody promise. Even if it means hiring a gang of men to hunt through every rattrap from here to China Basin."

V

Andrew Costain's offices were in a brick building on Geary Street that housed a dozen attorneys and half as many other professional men. The anteroom held a secretary's desk but no secretary; the bare desktop and dusty file cabinets behind it suggested that there hadn't been one in some while. A pair of neatly lettered and somewhat contradictory signs were affixed to one of two closed doors in the inside wall. The upper one proclaimed **Private**, the lower invited **Knock for Admittance**.

Quincannon knocked. Costain's whiskey baritone called him in. The lawyer sat behind a cluttered desk set before a wall covered with law books, among them what appeared to be a full set of Blackstone. More books and papers were scattered on dusty pieces of furniture. On another wall, next to a framed law degree, was a lithograph of John L. Sullivan in a fighting pose.

Costain's person was more tidy than his office; he wore an expensive tweed suit and a fancy striped vest, and, when he stood up, an elk's tooth gleamed at the end of a heavy gold watch chain. The successful image, however, was spoiled by his rum-blossom nose and a faint perfume of forty-rod whiskey that could be detected at fewer than ten paces. If Quincannon had been a prospective client, he would have thought twice about entrusting his legal business to Mr. Andrew Costain.

"Well, Quincannon, I expected you much sooner than this."

"At my convenience, your message said."

"It also offered you a financial advantage."

"So it did. For what service, Mister Costain?"

"That's rather obvious, isn't it, after last night? Sit down, Quincannon. Cigar? Drink?"

"Neither." He moved a heavy volume of Blackstone from the single client's chair and replaced it with his backside.

Costain asked: "Have you caught the scoundrel yet?"

"If you mean the housebreaker, no, not yet."

"Identified him?"

"Yes. It's only a matter of time until he's locked away in the city jail."

"How much time?"

"A day or two."

"How do you plan to catch him? While in the act?"

"Perhaps."

"Don't be ambiguous, man. I have a right to know what you're up to."

"My client is the Great Western Insurance Company," Quincannon said. "I need answer only to them."

"My name is on that list of potential victims, you said so last night. Naturally I'm concerned. Suppose he wasn't frightened off by his near capture at the Truesdales'? Suppose he's bold enough to try burgling my home next, even this very night? I can ill afford to have my house ransacked and valuables stolen. Those damned insurance people never pay off at full value."

"A legitimate fear."

"I want you to prevent that from happening. Hire you to prevent it. Watch my home every night until the thief is arrested, beginning tonight."

Quincannon said reluctantly: "There are other alternatives, you know, which would cost you nothing."

"Yes, yes, I know. Move our valuables to a safe place and simply stay home nights until the threat is ended. But we have too many possessions to haul away willy-nilly and too little time to do so. Even if we did remove everything of value, the burglar might still break in and vandalize the premises if he found nothing worth stealing. That has been known to happen, hasn't it?"

"It has, though not very often."

"I don't like the idea of my home being invaded in any case. And it damned well could be. My wife and I have separate appointments tonight and a joint one tomorrow evening that we're loathe to cancel. The house will be empty and fair game from seven until midnight or later both nights."

"You have no servants?"

"None that live in. And it would be useless to ask help from city police without certain knowledge of a crime to be committed."

"So it would."

"Well? There is no conflict of interest involved, after all."

True enough. If Costain wanted to pay him to do the same work for which he was being paid by Great Western Insurance, there was neither conflict nor a reasonable argument against it. The notion of another night or two hiding in shrubbery and risking pneumonia had no appeal, but minor hardships were part and parcel of the detective game. Besides, nothing warmed his Scot's blood like the fattening of the agency's bank account.

"You'll accept the job, then?"

"I will," Quincannon said blandly, "provided you're willing to pay an additional fee."

"What's that? For what?"

"Surveillance on your home is a job for two men."

"Why? You were alone at the Truesdales'."

"The Truesdale house has front and side entrances which could be watched by one man alone. Yours has front and rear entrances, therefore requiring a second operative."

"How is it you know my house?"

"I tabbed it up, along with the others on the list, the day I was hired."

"Tabbed it up?"

"Crook's argot. Paid visits and scrutinized the properties, the same as the housebreaker would have done to size up the lay."

Costain opened a desk drawer, removed a flask and a finger-marked glass, poured the glass half full, and sat, frowning while he nipped at it. At length the frown smoothed off and he drank the rest of his whiskey at a gulp. "Very well," he said. "How much will it cost me?"

Quincannon named a *per diem* figure, only slightly higher than his usual for a two-man operation. He cared little for Costain, but the dislike was not enough to warrant gouging the man unduly.

The amount induced the lawyer to pour himself a second drink. "That's damned close to extortion," he muttered.

"Hardly. My fees are standard."

"And non-negotiable, I suppose."

"Under all circumstances," Quincannon lied.

"Very well, then. How much in advance?"

"One day's fee in full."

"For services not yet rendered? No, by God! Half, and not a penny more."

Quincannon shrugged. Half in advance was more than he usually requested from his clients.

"You had better not fail me, Quincannon," Costain said as he wrote out a bank check. "If there is a repeat of your bungling at the Truesdales', you'll regret it. I promise you that."

"I did not bungle at the Truesdales'. What happened last night. . . ."

". . . wasn't your fault. Yes, I know. And if anything similar happens it won't be your fault again, no doubt."

Quincannon said—"You'll have your money's worth."—tucked the check into a waistcoat pocket, and left Costain to stew in his alcoholic juices.

The Geary Street address was not far from his own offices; he traveled the distance on foot at a brisk pace. San Francisco was a fine city, the more so on balmy days such as this one. The fresh salt smell from the bay, the rumble and clang of cable cars on Market Street, the booming horn of one of the fast coastal steamers as it drew into or away from the Embarcadero, the stately presence of the Ferry Building in the distance—he had yet to tire of any of it. It had been a banner day when he had been reassigned to San Francisco during his days with the United States Secret Service. The nation's capital had not been the same for him after his father, Thomas L. Quincannon, himself a fearless rival of Allen Pinkerton, succumbed to an assassin's bullet on the Baltimore docks; he had been ready for a change. His new home suited him as Washington, D.C. had suited his father. The same was true of the business of private investigation.

When he arrived at the building that housed Carpenter and Quincannon, Professional Detective Services, he was in high spirits. He whistled tunefully under his breath as he climbed the stairs to the second floor and approached the door to his offices. But he stopped when he saw the door

41

stood ajar by a few inches and heard the voice that emanated from within.

"I consider that a man's brain originally is like a little empty attic," the voice was declaiming, "and you have to stock it with such furniture as you choose. A fool takes in all the lumber of every sort that he comes across, so that the knowledge which might be useful to him gets crowded out, or at best is jumbled up with a lot of other things, so that he has a difficulty in laying his hands upon it. Now the skillful workman is very careful indeed as to what he takes in to his brain attic. He will have nothing but the tools which may help him in doing his work, but of these he has a large assortment, and all in the most perfect order. It is a mistake to think that little room has elastic walls and can distend to any extent. There comes a time when for every addition of knowledge you forget something that you knew before. It is of the highest importance, therefore, not to have useless facts elbowing out the useful ones."

Quincannon's cheerful smile turned upside down as he elbowed inside. The voice belonged to Sherlock Holmes.

VI

The Englishman was sitting comfortably in the client's chair in front of Sabina's desk, a gray cape draped over his narrow shoulders and an odd-looking cloth cap hiding his ears. The office was blue with smoke from the long, black, clay pipe he was smoking. Quincannon's nostrils twitched and pinched; the tobacco Holmes used might have been made from floor sweepings.

From the expression on Sabina's face, Holmes had had a rapt listener for his prattle about brain attics. This annoyed

Quincannon even more. He was not gentle in closing the door behind him, or gracious in his opening remark.

"I seem to have walked in on a lecture," he said to Sabina.

Her sharp look warned him to be civil. "Mister Holmes wasn't lecturing, he was simply answering a question. He really does have amazing powers of observation and deduction."

If it was possible to bow while sitting down, the Englishman managed it. "You're most kind, my dear Missus Carpenter."

Under his breath Quincannon muttered an unkindness.

"Why," Sabina said, "he wasn't here one minute before he knew about Adam."

"Adam? Who the deuce is Adam?"

"My new roommate."

"Your . . . *what?*"

"Oh, you needn't look so horrified. Adam is a cat."

"Kitten, in point of fact," Holmes said. "Three months old."

"Cat? You never told me you had a cat."

"Well, I've only had him two days," Sabina said. "Such a cute little fellow that I couldn't bring myself to turn him away when a neighbor brought him by."

"Rather a curious mix of Abyssinian and long-haired Siamese," Holmes announced.

"He was able to deduce that from a few wisps of fur on the hem of my skirt. Adam's approximate age, as well. Isn't that remarkable?"

"Stultifying," Quincannon said. "Have you written a monograph on breeds of cat as well as tobacco ash, Holmes?"

"No, but perhaps one day I shall."

"Which will doubtless earn you the mantle of recognized authority. What brought you here, may I ask?"

Sabina said: "Mister Holmes is interested in the inner workings of an American detective agency. And in the progress of our investigation into the house burglaries."

"Is he now. Why?"

"Now that I've finished my researches here," Holmes said, "I fear I've grown bored with conventional tourist activities. San Francisco is a cosmopolitan city, to be sure, but its geographical, cultural, and historical attractions have decidedly limited appeal."

"What researches?"

Holmes smiled enigmatically. "They are of an esoteric nature, of no interest to the average person."

Another bumptious statement. Quincannon shed his Chesterfield, went to open the window behind his desk. The Englishman's strong, acrid tobacco was making his head swim.

"The time of my self-imposed exile has almost ended," Holmes was saying to Sabina. "Soon I shall return to my former life in London. Crime and the criminal mind challenge my intellect, give zest to my life. I've been away from the game too long."

"I can't imagine leaving it in the first place," Quincannon said.

"I daresay there were mitigating factors."

"Not for any reason, with or without mitigating factors."

Their gazes locked, struck a spark or two. Sabina asked quickly: "You've been gone most of the day, John. What news?"

"Yes," Holmes said, "were you able to locate your panny-man?"

Quincannon ignored the Englishman, fixed his partner with a disapproving eye. "You've been confiding some of our business, I see."

"I confided little except Dodger Brown's name. You seem to have revealed most details about the case yourself, last night."

"If I did, it was from necessity."

"*Did* you find the Dodger?"

"Not yet, but it's only a matter of time."

Holmes puffed up a great cloud of smoke and said through it, his eyes agleam: "Doctor Axminster provided a brief tour of the Barbary Coast shortly after my arrival, but it was superficial and hardly enlightening. I should like to see it as I've seen Limehouse in London, from the perspective of a consulting detective. Foul dives, foul deeds! My blood races at the prospect."

Blasted rattlepate, Quincannon thought. *The man's daft as a church mouse.*

"Would you permit me to join you on your next visit? Introduce me to the district's hidden intrigues, some of its more colorful denizens . . . the dance hall queen known as The Galloping Cow, Emperor Norton, the odd fellow who allows himself to be beaten up for money?"

"Emperor Norton is dead, and Oofty Goofty soon will be if he allows one more thump on his cranium with a baseball bat. Besides, I'm a detective, not a tour guide."

"Tut, tut. It's knowledge I'm interested in, not sensation. In return, perhaps I can be of assistance in tracking down Dodger Brown and the stolen loot."

"I don't need assistance, yours or anyone else's. I have no intention. . . ."

Quincannon broke off because a pleasantly evil thought had popped into his head. He nurtured and fondled it for a few moments. Then he said to Sabina: "I stopped by Andrew Costain's law offices on my way here."

"Yes? What exactly did he want?"

"To have his home put under surveillance until Dodger Brown is caught."

"You didn't accept?"

"I did, and why not? There's no conflict of interest in taking payment from more than one client to perform the same task, as Costain himself pointed out."

"Still, it doesn't seem quite ethical. . . ."

"Ethics be damned. A fee is a fee for services rendered, and that includes providing peace of mind to nervous citizens. Eh, Holmes?"

"Indubitably."

"We're to begin tonight," Quincannon told Sabina. "Costain's home is near South Park, not as large a property as banker Truesdale's but nonetheless substantial, and with both a front and rear entrance. I explained to Costain that proper surveillance will require two operatives, and he agreed to the extra fee."

"John," she said, "you're not going to suggest . . . ?"

Ignoring her, he said to the Englishman: "There are a number of operatives I could call upon, but I wonder, given your interest in this case and your eagerness to return to the game, if you might be willing to join me at the task?"

Another obnoxious cloud erupted from Holmes's pipe. "Splendid suggestion! I would be honored. As for payment for my services, I ask only that you acquaint me with the Barbary Coast as you know it."

If Holmes hadn't suggested this, Quincannon would have. Now the additional fee would fatten the agency's coffers in its entirety. He said: "Agreed. You'll see the Coast as few ever have." Or would want to.

Holmes smiled.

Quincannon smiled.

Sabina sighed and looked from one to the other as if she thought they were both daft as church mice.

VII

During Quincannon's two-year attempt to drown his conscience in demon rum, Hoolihan's Saloon on Second Street had been his favorite watering hole. Its clientele consisted mainly of small merchants, office workers, tradesmen, drummers, and a somewhat rougher element up from the waterfront. No city leaders came there on their nightly rounds, as they did to the Palace Hotel bar, Pop Sullivan's Hoffman Café, and the other first-class saloons along the city's Cocktail Route; no judges, politicians, bankers—Samuel Truesdale had likely never set foot through its swinging doors—or gay young blades in their striped trousers, fine cravats, and brocaded waistcoats. Hoolihan's had no crystal chandeliers, fancy mirrors, expensive oil paintings, white-coated barmen, or elaborate free lunch. It was dark and bare by comparison, sawdust thick-scattered on the floor and the only glitter and sparkle coming from the shine of its old-style gaslights on the ranks of bottles and glasses along the backbar. Its hungry drinkers dined not on crab legs and oysters on the half shell, but on corned beef, strong cheese, rye bread, and tubs of briny pickles.

Quincannon had gravitated there because Hoolihan's was a short cable car ride from his rooms on Leavenworth and because staff and clientele both respected the solitary drinker's desire for privacy. Even after taking the pledge, he continued to patronize it because it was an honest place, made for those who sought neither bombast nor trouble. Far fewer lies were told in Hoolihan's than in the rarified atmosphere of the Palace bar, he suspected, and far fewer dark deeds were hatched.

He had arranged to meet Sherlock Holmes there at seven o'clock. He arrived a few minutes early, claimed a place at the bar near the entrance. Ben Joyce, the head barman, greeted him in his mildly profane fashion. "What'll it be tonight, you bloody Scotsman? Coffee or clam juice?"

"Clam juice, and leave out the arsenic this time."

"Hah. As if I'd waste good rats-bane on the likes of you."

Ben brought him a steaming mug of Hoolihan's special broth. Quincannon sipped, smoked, and listened to the ebb and flow of conversation around him. Men came in, singly and in pairs, men drifted out. The hands on the massive Seth Thomas clock over the backbar moved forward to seven o'clock. And seven-oh-five. And seven-ten. . . .

Annoyance nibbled at Quincannon. Where the devil was he? He'd considered himself a sly fox for his conscription of Holmes, but mayhap he'd outsmarted himself. If the fellow was untrustworthy. . . .

Someone moved in next to him, jostling his arm. A gruff Cockney voice said: "Yer standing in me way, mate."

Quincannon turned to glare at the voice's owner. Tall, thin ragamuffin dressed in patched trousers and a threadbare pea jacket, a cap pulled down low on his forehead. He opened his mouth to make a sharp retort, then closed it again and took a closer look at the man. Little surprised him any more, but he was a bit taken aback by what he saw.

"Holmes?" he said.

"At yer service, mate."

"What's the purpose of that get-up?"

"It seemed appropriate for the night's mission," Holmes said in his normal voice. His eyes, peering up from under the brim of his cap, were mischievous. "Disguise has served me well during my career, and the opportunity has not presented itself in some time. I must say I enjoy play-acting. It has been said, perhaps truly, that the stage lost a consummate actor when I decided to become a detective."

Quincannon, with an effort, forebore comment. Quickly he ushered Holmes outside and into a hansom waiting nearby. The Englishman had no more to say on the subject of disguises, but, as the hack rattled along the cobblestones to Mission and on toward Rincon Hill, he put forth a slew of questions on the night's venture, the history and habits of Dodger Brown, and the various methods employed by burglars in the United States. The man was obsessed with details and minutiae on every conceivable subject.

Quincannon answered as best he could at first, then lapsed into monosyllabic replies in the hope that Holmes would wind down and be quiet. This was not to be. The Englishman kept up a running colloquy on a variety of esoteric topics from the remarkable explorations of a Norwegian named Sigerson to the latest advances in chemistry and other sciences to the inner workings and possible improvements of horseless carriages. He even knew (although Quincannon could not for the life of him figure how, and Holmes refused to elaborate) that an ex-burglar living in Warsaw, Illinois manufactured burglar tools, advertised them as novelties in the *Police Gazette*, and sold them for ten dollars the set.

His monologue ceased, mercifully, when they departed the hack two blocks from Andrew Costain's home. It was another night made for prowling, restless streamers of cloud playing peek-a-boo games with stars and the scythe-blade moon. The neighborhood, the first of San Francisco's fashionable residential districts, had fallen into disfavor in 1869, when Second Street was carved through the west edge of Rincon Hill to connect downtown with the southern waterfront. Now it was on the shabby side, although far from the "new slum, a place of solitary ancient houses and butt ends of streets," as it had been unfairly dubbed by that insolent writer fellow, R. L. Stevenson.

Many of the houses they passed showed light, but the Costain house, near South Park, was dark except for a porch globe. It was not as large as the Truesdale pile, but its front and rear yards were spacious and contained almost as many plants, trees, and shadowy hiding places.

Holmes peered intently through the row of iron pickets into the front yard as they strolled by. "Which of us will be stationed here?" he asked.

"You will. I've a spot picked out at the rear."

"Splendid. The *mucronulatum,* perhaps. Or . . . ah, yes, even better. A *Juniperus chinensis Corymbosa Variegata,* I do believe."

"What are you talking about?"

"Shrubbery."

"Eh?"

"*Mucronulatum* is the species more commonly known as rhododendron. Quite a healthy specimen there by that garden bench."

"And what, pray, is Jupiter chinchin thrombosa?"

"*Juniperus chinensis Corymbosa Variegata,*" Holmes corrected sententiously. "One of the more handsome and sturdy varieties of juniper shrub. Its flowers are a variegated creamy yellow and its growth regular, without twisted branches, and generally of no more than ten feet in height. I thought at first that it might be a *chenisis corymbosa,* a close cousin, but the *chenisis corymbosa* grows to a greater height, often above fifteen feet."

Quincannon had nothing to say to that.

"I've decided the *corymbosa variegata* will afford the best concealment," Holmes said. "Without obstructing vision, of course. But I should like to see the rear of the property as well, if you have no objection. So that I may have a more complete knowledge of the . . . ah . . . lay. That is the American term?"

"It is."

"I find your idiom fascinating," Holmes said. "One day I shall make a study of American slang."

"And write a monograph about it, no doubt."

"Or an article for one of the London popular journals."

They reached the end of the block and circled around into a deserted carriageway. When they came to the rear of the Costain property, Holmes peered in as intently as he had in front and then asked where Quincannon would station himself. "That tree there on your left," Quincannon lied. "I don't happen to know its Latin or its English name, but I expect you do."

"*Taxus brevifolia,*" Holmes said promptly, "the Pacific yew."

Quincannon ground his teeth. The prospect of two or three more nights in the Englishman's company, not to mention a day trip to the low dives of the Barbary Coast, was about as appealing as having one of his teeth pulled without benefit of nitrous oxide. Uncharitably he decided that Holmes's biographer and alleged good friend, Dr. Watson, must be either a saint or a long-suffering, hero-worshipping twit.

He said: "If you've seen enough, we'll take our positions now."

"Quite enough. A long low whistle if our man should appear, and we'll then join forces at the fountain in the side yard. Yes?"

"Your memory is as keen as your conversation."

Holmes said—"Indeed."—and hurried on his way.

Quincannon returned to the gate that gave access to the Costain property. He made sure he was still alone and unobserved, then stepped through the shadows alongside a small carriage barn. The surveillance spot he had picked out on his earlier tabbing was a shed set at an angle midway between house and barn. Not only did it provide a viewpoint of the rear yard, gate, and part of the side yard, but also some shelter from the wind and the night's chill. The thought of Sherlock Holmes shivering among the chenisis whosis in front would warm him even more.

He made his way through heavy shadow to the shed, eased the door open and himself inside. The interior was cramped with stacks of cordwood and a jumble of gardening implements. By careful feel with his hands he found that the stack nearest the door was low enough and sturdy enough to afford a seat, if he were careful not to move about too much. He lowered himself onto the wood. Even with the door wide open, he was in such darkness that he couldn't be seen from outside. Yet his range of vision was mostly unimpeded and aided by star shine and patchy moonlight.

He judged that it was well after seven by now. Andrew Costain had told him that his wife was due home no later than ten-thirty, and that he himself would return by midnight. The odds were long against another break-in on the heels of the Truesdale misadventure. And three and a half hours was little enough discomfort and boredom in exchange for the double fee Carpenter and Quincannon, Professional Detective Services would collect for this night's business.

As it turned out, he was wrong on both counts.

His wait lasted less than two hours. He was on his feet, flexing his limbs to ease them of cold and cramp, when to his startlement he spied the interloper. A shadow among shadows, moving crosswise from his left—the same silent, flitting approach he had observed on the banker's property last night. Dodger Brown was evidently bolder and more greedy and foolish than experience had taught him. Bully! The sooner he nabbed the scruff, the sooner Carpenter and Quincannon would collect from Great Western Insurance. And the sooner he would be rid of Mr. Sherlock Holmes.

Quincannon rubbed his gloved hands together, watching the shadow's progress toward the rear of the house. Pause, drift, pause again at the rear end of the porch. Up and over the railing there, briefly silhouetted: same small figure dressed in dark cap and clothing. Across to the door; at work there for just a few seconds. The door opened, closed again behind the intruder.

He spent several seconds readying his dark lantern, just in case. When one of the wind-herded clouds blotted the moon, he emerged from the shed and went laterally to the bole of tree a dozen rods from the house. He was about to give the signal whistle when a low ululation came from the front yard. What the devil? He answered in kind, paused and whistled again. In a matter of moments he spied movement approaching. Holmes seemed to have an uncanny sense of direction in the dark; he came in an unerring line straight to where Quincannon stood.

"Why did you whistle, man?" Quincannon demanded in

a fierce whisper. "You couldn't have seen. . . ."

"Andrew Costain is here."

"*What?*"

"Arrived not three minutes ago, alone in a trap."

"Blasted fool! He couldn't have chosen a worse time. You didn't stop him from going inside?"

"He seemed in a great hurry and I saw no purpose in revealing myself. Dodger Brown is also here, I assume?"

"Already inside through the rear door, not four minutes ago."

"Inside with us, too, Quincannon!" Holmes said urgently. "We've not a moment to lose!"

But it was already too late. In that instant a percussive report came from the house, muffled but unmistakable.

Holmes said: "Pistol shot."

Quincannon said: "Hell and damn!"

Both men broke into a run. Quincannon had no need to order the Englishman to cover the front door; Holmes immediately veered off in that direction. The Navy Colt and the dark lantern were both at the ready when he reached the rear porch. Somewhere inside, another door slammed. He ran up the steps to the door, thumbed open the lantern's bull's-eye lens, and shouldered his way through.

The thin beam showed him a utility porch, an opening into a broad kitchen. His foot struck something as he started ahead; the light revealed it to be a wooden wedge, of the sort used to prop open doors. Quincannon shut the door and toed the wedge tightly under the sill—a safeguard against swift escape that took only a clutch of seconds.

Two or three additional sounds reached his ears as he plunged ahead, none distinguishable or close by. The beam picked out an electric switch on the kitchen wall; he turned it to flood the room with light. Empty. Likewise an adjoining dining room. His twitching nose picked up the acrid smell of burnt gunpowder, led him into a central hallway. He flooded the hall with more electric light, eased past two closed doors to a third at the end, where another hallway intersected this one. The powder smell was strongest there.

He paused to listen. Heavy, crackling silence. He moved ahead to where he could see along the intersecting hall, found it deserted, and stepped up to the third door to try the latch. Locked from within; there was no key on this side.

He rapped sharply on the panel, called out: "Costain? John Quincannon. It's safe for you to come out now."

No response. But more sounds came from the front of the house—a heavy dragging noise, as of a piece of furniture being moved.

"Costain?" Louder this time.

Silence from behind the door.

Movement at the corner of his eye swung him around and brought the Navy to bear on the intersecting hallway. Sherlock Holmes was but a short distance away, approaching as noiselessly as a cat stalking prey. Quincannon lowered his weapon, said as Holmes hurried up: "A sign of either man?"

"None."

"One or both must be on the other side of this door. Locked from the inside."

"If the intruder is elsewhere and attempts to leave by way of the front door, he'll first have to move a heavy oak chair, and we'll hear him."

"I wedged the rear door shut for the same reason."

Quincannon holstered the Navy, then backed off two steps and flung the full weight of his body against the door panel. This rash action succeeded only in bruising flesh, jarring bone and teeth. Fortunately for Sherlock Holmes, he made no comment; he was standing with his head cocked in a listening attitude. Grumbling, Quincannon gathered himself and drove the flat of his foot against the wood just above the latch. Two more kicks were necessary to splinter the wood, tear the locking mechanism loose, and send the door wobbling inward.

Only a few scant inches inward, however, before it bound up against something heavy and inert on the floor.

Quincannon shoved hard against the panel until he was able to widen the opening enough to wedge his body through. The room was dark except for faint patches that marked uncurtained windows at the far end. He swept his hand along the wall, located a switch, turned it. The flood of electric light revealed what lay on the carpeted floor just inside the door.

The body was that of Andrew Costain, sprawled face down, both arms outflung, the one visible eye wide open. Dead, and no mistake. Blood stained the back of his cheviot coat, the sleeve of his left forearm. Scorch marks blackened the sleeve as well.

The room, evidently Costain's study, was otherwise empty. Two drawers in a roll-top desk stood open, another had been yanked out and upended on the desk top. Papers littered the surface, the floor around the desk. Also on the floor, between the corpse and the desk, were two other items: a new-looking revolver, and a brassbound valuables case that appeared to have been pried open and was now plainly empty.

Holmes crowded in. Both men swept the room with keen gazes, after which Quincannon crossed to examine the windows. Both were of the casement type, with hook latches firmly in place; Dodger Brown hadn't gotten out that way.

Still hiding somewhere in the house, or possibly gone by now through another window.

When Quincannon turned, he was confronted by the sight of Sherlock Holmes on one knee, hunched over the corpse like a strange, lank bird, peering through a large magnifying glass at the wound in Costain's back. His lean hawk's face was darkly flushed, his brows drawn into two hard black lines. A small smile appeared as he lifted his head. His eyes showed a steely glitter.

"Interesting," he said. "Quite."

"What is?"

"Andrew Costain was stabbed to death."

"Stabbed? Not shot?"

"Shot, too. Two separate and distinct wounds. The superficial one in his forearm was made by a bullet. The fatal wound was made by an instrument at least eight inches in length and quite sharp. A stiletto, I should say. The blow was struck by a right-handed person approximately five and a half feet tall, at an upward angle of perhaps fifteen degrees."

Blasted know-it-all!

Quincannon located the lead pellet that had passed through Costain's arm in the cushion of an armchair near the desk, then picked up the revolver. It was a Forehand & Wadsworth .38 caliber, its nickel-plated finish free of marks of any kind. He sniffed the barrel to confirm that it had been recently fired, opened the breech for a squint inside. All of the chambers were empty. He was about to return the weapon to the carpet when Holmes stepped up, took it from his hand, and commenced to peer at it through his glass.

Glowering, Quincannon left the study to search the premises. Not long afterward, Holmes did the same. The results were rather astonishing. They found no sign of Dodger

Brown, and yet every window, upstairs and down, was firmly latched. Furthermore, the wedge Quincannon had kicked under the back door was still in place, as was the heavy chair Holmes had dragged over to block the front door. Those were the only two doors that provided an exit from the house.

"How the deuce could he have gotten out?" Quincannon said. "Even the cellar door in the kitchen is locked tight. And I doubt there was enough time for him to slip away *before* we entered."

"Dear me, no. You or I would have seen him."

"Well, he managed it somehow."

"So it would seem. A miraculous double escape, in fact."

"Double escape?"

"From a locked room, and then from a sealed house." Holmes smiled one of his enigmatic smiles. "According to Doctor Axminster, you are adept at solving seemingly impossible crimes. How then did Dodger Brown manage either a single or double escape trick? Why was Andrew Costain shot as well as stabbed? Why was the pistol left in the locked study and the bloody stiletto taken away? And why was the study door locked in the first place? A pretty puzzle, eh, Quincannon? One to challenge the deductive mind."

Quincannon muttered five short, colorful words, none of them remotely of a deductive nature.

VIII

As much as Quincannon disliked and mistrusted the city police, the circumstances of the crime were such that notifying them was unavoidable. He telephoned the Hall of Justice on the instrument in Costain's study. After that he paced and cogitated, to no reasonable conclusion. Holmes examined the corpse again, the carpet in both the study and the hallway (crawling on his hands and knees), and any number of other things through his glass. Now and then he muttered aloud to himself: "More data! I can't make bricks without clay!" and "Hallo! That's more like it!" and "Ah, plain as a pikestaff!" Neither had anything more to say to the other. It was as if a gauntlet had been thrown down, a tacit challenge issued—which in fact was the case. They were two bloodhounds on the scent, no longer working in consort, but as competitors in an undeclared contest of wills.

The police arrived in less than half an hour, what for them was quick dispatch. They were half a dozen in number, along with a handful of reporters representing the *Daily Alta*, the *Call*, and San Francisco's other newspapers, who were made to wait outside—half as many of both breeds as there would have been if the murder of a prominent attorney had happened on Nob Hill or Russian Hill. The inspector in charge was a beefy, red-faced Prussian named Kleinhoffer, who Quincannon knew slightly and condoned not in the slightest. Kleinhoffer was both stupid and corrupt, a lethal combination, and a political toady besides. His opinion of fly cops was on a par with Quincannon's opinion of him.

His first comment was: "Involved in another killing, eh, Quincannon? What's your excuse this time?"

Quincannon explained, briefly, the reason he was there. He omitted mention of Dodger Brown by name, using the term "unknown burglar" instead and catching Sherlock Holmes's eye as he spoke so the Englishman would say nothing to contradict him. He was not about to chance losing a fee—small chance though it was, the police being a generally inept bunch—by providing information that might allow them to stumble across the Dodger ahead of him.

Kleinhoffer sneered: "Some fancy fly cop. You're sure he's not still somewhere in the house?"

"Sure enough."

"We'll see about that." He gestured to a uniformed sergeant, who stepped forward. "Mahoney, you and your men search the premises, top to bottom."

"Yes, sir."

Kleinhoffer's beady gaze settled on Holmes, ran over both his face and his disguise. He demanded: "Who're you?"

"S. Holmes, of London, England. A temporary associate of the Carpenter and Quincannon agency."

"A limey, eh?" Kleinhoffer turned to Quincannon. "Picking your operatives off the docks these days, are you?"

"If I am, it's none of your concern."

"None of your guff. Where's the stiff?"

"In the study."

Kleinhoffer gave Andrew Costain's remains a cursory examination. "Shot and stabbed both," he said. "You didn't tell me that. What the hell happened here tonight?"

Quincannon's account, given in deliberate detail, heightened the inspector's apoplectic color, narrowed his eyes to slits. Any crime more complicated than a Barbary Coast mugging invariably confused him, and the evident facts in this case threatened to tie a permanent knot in his brain.

He shook his head, as if trying to shake loose cobwebs, and snapped: "None of that makes a damn' bit of sense."

"Sense or not, that is exactly what took place."

"You there, limey. He leave anything out?"

"Tut, tut," Holmes said. "I am an Englishman, sir, a

British subject . . . not a limey."

"I don't care if you're the president of England.
Quincannon leave anything out or didn't he?"

"He did not. His recreation of events was exact in every
detail."

"So you say. I say it couldn't've happened the way you
tell it."

"Nonetheless, it did, though what seems to have tran-
spired is not necessarily what actually happened. What we
are dealing with here is illusion and obfuscation."

Kleinhoffer wrapped an obscene noun in a casing of disgust. After which he stooped to pick up the Forehand &
Wadsworth revolver. He sniffed the barrel and checked the
chambers, as Quincannon had done, then dropped the
weapon into his coat pocket. He was examining the empty
valuables case when Sergeant Mahoney entered the room.

"No sign of him in the house," he reported.

"Back door still wedged shut?"

"Yes, sir."

"Then he must've managed to slip out the front door
while these two fly cops weren't looking."

"I beg to differ," Holmes said. He mentioned the heavy
chair. "It was not moved until your arrival, Inspector, by
Quincannon and myself. Even if it had been, I would surely
have heard the sounds. My hearing is preternaturally
acute."

Kleinhoffer said the rude word again.

Mahoney said: "Missus Costain is here."

"What's that?"

"The victim's wife. Missus Costain. She just come
home."

"Why the devil didn't you say so? Bring her in here."

The sergeant did as directed. Penelope Costain was styl-

61

ishly dressed in a lacy blouse, flounced skirt, and fur-trimmed cloak, her brown curls tucked under a hat adorned with an ostrich plume. She took one look at her husband's remains, and her face whitened to the shade of the feather; she shuddered violently, began to sway. Mahoney caught one arm to steady her. Quincannon took hold of the other and they helped her to one of the chairs.

She drew several deep breaths, fanned herself with one hand. "I . . . I'm all right," she said then. Her gaze touched the body again, pulled away. "Poor Andrew. He was a brave man . . . he must have fought terribly for his life."

"We'll get the man who did it," Kleinhoffer promised foolishly.

She nodded. "Can't you . . . cover him with something?"

"Mahoney. Find a cloth."

"Yes, sir."

Mrs. Costain nibbled at a broken fingernail, peering up at the faces ringed above her. "Is that you, Mister Holmes? What are you doing here, dressed that way?"

"He was working with me," Quincannon said.

"With you? Two detectives in tandem failed to prevent this . . . this outrage?"

"None of what happened was our fault."

She said bitterly: "That is the same statement you made two nights ago. Nothing, no tragedy, is ever your fault, evidently."

Kleinhoffer was still holding the empty valuables case. He extended it to the widow, saying: "This was on the floor, Missus Costain."

"Yes. My husband kept it in his desk."

"What was in it?"

"Twenty-dollar gold pieces," she answered, "a dozen or so. And the more valuable among my jewelry . . . a diamond brooch, a pair of diamond earrings, a pearl necklace, several other pieces."

"Worth how much, would you say?"

"I don't know . . . several thousand dollars."

She looked again at Quincannon, this time with open hostility. Kleinhoffer did the same. He said: "You and Holmes were here the whole time, and still you let that yegg kill Mister Costain and then get away with all those valuables . . . right under your damn' noses. What've you got to say for yourselves?"

Quincannon had nothing to say. Neither did Sherlock Holmes.

IX

It was well past midnight when Quincannon finally trudged wearily up the stairs to his rooms. After Kleinhoffer had finally finished with him, the newspapermen had descended—on him but not Holmes, who had managed to slip away. Quincannon had been pleased to assist the Englishman in avoiding publicity; in his comments to the reporters, he had referred to him as a "hired operative" and, with relish, an "underling".

He donned his nightshirt and crawled into bed, but the night's jumbled events plagued his mind and refused to let him sleep. At length he lit his bedside lamp, picked up a copy of Walt Whitman's *Sea-Drift*. Reading always seemed to free his brain of clutter, to permit a settling and organizing of his thoughts. Usually Whitman or Emily Dickinson or James Lowell accomplished the task, but not tonight. He switched reading matter to *Drunkards and Curs: The Truth About Demon Rum*. He had once been hired by the True Christian Temperance Society to catch an embezzler, and this had led him to his second reading and collecting interest: temperance tracts. Not because he was now a teetotaler himself, but because he found their highly inflammatory rhetoric both amusing and soothing.

Drunkards and Curs did the trick. At the end of two turgid chapters his mental processes were in proper condition for cudgeling and surmising. The result of this brainwork, after another hour or so, lifted his spirits and permitted him a too-short rest.

He awoke not long past seven, allowed himself a hasty breakfast, and within an hour was at the agency offices. For once he was the first to arrive. No sooner had he unlocked the door and stepped inside than the telephone bell jangled. When he answered, a rough and unfamiliar voice said "Duff's Curio Shop," repeated the name, and immediately disconnected.

A wolf's smile transformed Quincannon's mouth. Another worry, small though it was, had now been reduced to a trifle and the fogbound morning was considerably brighter. He replaced the handset, went to coax steam heat from the radiator; on mornings such as this, the offices were as damp and chill as a cave. While he was thus engaged, Sabina arrived.

"Up bright and early this morning, John," she said. Then, as she removed her straw boater, she took a closer look at him. "But not bushy-tailed, I see. Another sleepless night?"

"For the most part."

"Not because of an eventful night at the Costain home?"

"Unfortunately, yes. Eventful as all get-out."

"Another attempted burglary so soon?"

"Not attempted . . . successful."

Sabina was not easily surprised; the high lift of her eyebrows as he unfolded the tale was as much marvelment as she ever exhibited. Her only comment was: "It all seems fantastic."

"That sums it in a nutshell."

"What does Mister Holmes think?"

"Holmes? Why should you care what he thinks?"

"I was only. . . ."

"Why don't you ask me what I think? I'm in charge of this case, not Sherlock Holmes. This is my bailiwick, not his. Or do you actually believe the bunkum that he is the world's greatest detective?"

"Calm yourself, John. I wasn't suggesting he's a better sleuth, or more likely than you to get to the bottom of the mystery." She fixed him with one of her analytical looks. "It sounds as though you're threatened by the man."

"Threatened? By the likes of that gasbag?"

"You've no reason to be."

"Exactly. No reason at all."

"I was merely wondering if you'd had a discussion with him, shared thoughts and ideas."

"I don't need his thoughts and ideas to unravel this puzzle."

"Does that mean you have a theory?"

"I have. A good, strong one." In fact it was still a bit on the amorphous side, but she needn't know that.

"Well?"

"I'll need a few more facts before I'm ready to discuss it, facts which you can obtain for me. Data on Andrew Costain, for one, with emphasis on his financial status. And second, whether he purchased a handgun within the past two or three days . . . specifically, a Thirty-Eight-caliber Forehand and Wadsworth revolver. If so, it was likely in a gun shop in the vicinity of his law offices."

"And what will you be doing?"

"Hunting Dodger Brown. We've a lead now, courtesy of Ezra Bluefield by way of one of his henchmen." He told her of the telephone message.

"Ah," she said, "our old friend Luther Duff."

"One of the easier eggs to crack in the city. Dodger Brown couldn't have picked a better fence man, for our purposes."

"Assuming Duff knows his whereabouts. The hide-out must be deep, else Bluefield's contacts would have ferreted it out as well. Time is against us now, John. If the Dodger has begun to fence the loot from his burglaries, it must mean he's preparing to go on the lammas."

Quincannon said darkly: "The only place that yegg is going is to a cell in city prison."

"On your way then. With luck, you'll have Dodger Brown and I'll have the Costain data before close of business."

He nodded and reached for his derby. With luck, he would also have the solution to the murder and disappearance before the end of the day. Yes, by Godfrey, and the great pleasure of using it to spit in the eye of Mr. Sherlock Holmes.

X

Luther Duff's Curio Shop was crowded among similar establishments in the second block of McAllister Street west of Van Ness. It contained, according to its proprietor: "bric-a-brac and curios of every type and description, from every culture and every nation . . . the new, the old, the mild, the exotic." In short, it was full of junk. This was Quincannon's fourth visit to the place, all on professional business, and he had yet to see a single customer. It may have been that Duff sold some of his fare now and then, but, if so, it was by accident and with little or no effort on his part. Where he had procured his inventory was a mystery; all that anyone knew for sure was that he had it and seldom if ever added new items to the dusty, moldering stock.

Duff's primary profession was receiver of stolen goods. Burglars, box men, pickpockets, and other scruffs far and wide beat a steady path to his door. Like other fence men, he professed to offer his fellow thieves a square deal: half of what he expected to realize on the resale of any particular item. In fact, his notion of fifty-fifty was akin to putting a lead dollar on a Salvation Army tambourine and asking for fifty cents change. He took a seventy-five percent cut of most spoils, an even higher percentage from the more gullible and desperate among his suppliers. Stolen weapons of all types were his specialty—often enough at an eighty or ninety percent profit. A Tenderloin hockshop might offer a thief more cash, but hockshop owners put their marks on pistols, marks that had been known to lead police agencies straight to the source. Hockshop owners were thus considered hangman's handmaidens, and crooks stayed shy of them, preferring smaller but safer profits from men like Luther Duff.

Despite being well known in the trade, Duff had somehow managed to avoid prosecution. This was both a strong advertisement and his Achilles heel. He had a horror of arrest and imprisonment, and was subject to intimidation as a result. Quincannon was of the opinion that Duff would sell his mother, if he had one, and his entire line of relatives rather than spend a single night at the mercy of a city prison guard.

A bell above the door jingled unmusically as Quincannon stepped into the shop. On the instant, the combined smells of dust, mildew, and slow decay pinched his nostrils. He made his way slowly through the dimly lighted interior, around and through an amazing hodgepodge of furniture that included a Chinese wardrobe festooned with fire-breathing dragons, a Tyrolean pine coffer, a Spanish refectory table, a brassbound "pirate treasure" chest from Madagascar. He passed shelves of worm-ridden books, an assortment of corpses that had once been clocks, a stuffed and molting weasel, an artillery bugle, a ship's sextant, and a broken marble tombstone with the name Horse-Shy Halloran chiseled into its face.

When he neared the long counter at the rear, a set of musty damask drapes parted and Luther Duff emerged, grinning. He was short, round, balding, fiftyish, and about as appetizing as a tainted oyster. He wore shyness and venality as openly as the garters on his sleeves and the money-lender's eyeshade across his forehead. The grin and the suddenness of his appearance made Quincannon think, as always, of a troll jumping out in front of an unwary traveler.

"Hello, hello, hello," the troll said. "What can I do for . . . *awk!*"

The strangled-chicken noise was the result of his having recognized Quincannon. The grin vanished in a wash of nervous fear. He stood stiffly and darted looks everywhere but across the counter into Quincannon's eyes.

"How are you, Luther?" Quincannon asked pleasantly.

"Ah . . . well and good, well and good."

"No health problems, I trust?"

"No, no, none, fit as a fiddle."

"Sound of body, pure of heart?"

"Ah, well, ah. . . ."

"But it's a harsh and uncertain world we live in, eh, Luther? Illness can strike any time. Accidents, likewise."

"Accidents?"

"Terrible, crippling accidents. Requiring a long stay in the hospital."

It was cold in the shop, but Duff's face was already damp. He produced a dark-flecked handkerchief, twitchily began to mop his brow.

"Of course, there are worse things even than illness and accident. Worse for some, that is. Such as those who suffer from claustrophobia."

"Claustro . . . what?"

"The terrible fear of being trapped in small enclosed spaces. A prison cell, for instance."

"*Gahh,*" the troll said. A shudder passed through him.

"Such a man would suffer greatly under those circumstances. I would hate to see it happen, the more so when it could be easily avoided."

"Ah . . ."

Quincannon simulated a tolerant smile. "Well, no more of that, eh? We'll move along to my reason for calling this morning. I'm after a bit of information I believe you can supply."

"Ah. . . ."

"It happens that I have urgent business with a lad named Dodger Brown. However, he seems to have dropped from sight."

"Dodger Brown?"

"The same. Wine dump habitué, gambler, and burglar by trade. You've had recent dealings with him, I understand."

"Recent dealings? No, you're mistaken."

"Now, now, Luther. Prison cells are cold and unpleasant, remember. And very, very small."

Duff fidgeted. "What . . . ah . . . what business do you have with him?"

"Mine and none of yours. All you need to do is tell me where I can find him."

"Ah. . . ."

"You must have some idea of his whereabouts." Quincannon let the smile slip away, his voice harden. "It wouldn't do for you to tax my patience."

"Oh . . . ah . . . I wouldn't, I won't," Duff said. The tip of his tongue flicked over thin lips. "An idea, perhaps. A possibility. You won't say where you heard?"

"No one need know of our little talk but us."

"Well . . . ah . . . he has a cousin, a fisherman called Salty Jim."

"Does he now." This was news to Quincannon; there was nothing in Dodger Brown's dossier about a living relative.

Duff said: "The Dodger has been known to bunk with him from time to time. So . . . ah . . . so I've heard on the earie."

"Where does this Salty Jim hang his cap? Fisherman's Wharf?"

"No. Across the bay . . . the Oakland City Wharf. He . . . ah . . . he's involved in the oyster trade."

"The name of his boat?"

"Something with *Oyster* in it. That's all I can tell you."

"Good enough," Quincannon said. "Now we'll move along to other matters. Did you sell the Dodger a revolver, new or old, recently?"

"Revolver? No. Absolutely not."

"That had better not be a lie."

"It's not! I swear I sold him no weapon of any kind."

"So he took only cash for whatever goods he brought you."

"I don't . . . ah . . . know what you mean. He came to see me, yes, but it was only to discuss selling certain property. . . ."

Quincannon smiled again, drew his Navy Colt, and laid the weapon on the countertop between them. "You were saying?"

"*Awk.*"

"No, that wasn't it. You were about to identify the items you purchased from Dodger Brown. In fact, in the spirit of co-operation and good fellowship between us, you were about to show me these items."

The troll swallowed in a way that was remarkably like a cow swallowing its cud. He twitched, looked at the pistol, nibbled at his lower lip like a rat nibbling cheese.

Quincannon picked up the Navy and held it loosely in his hand, the barrel aimed in the general direction of Duff's right eye. "My time is valuable, Luther," he said. "And yours is fast running out."

The troll turned abruptly and stepped through the drapery. Quincannon vaulted the counter, followed him into an incredibly cluttered office lighted by an oil lamp. A farrago of items covered the surface of a battered roll-top desk; boxes and wrappings littered the floor; piles of curios teetered precariously on a pair of claw-foot tables. In one corner was a large and fairly new Mosler safe. Duff glanced back at Quincannon, noted his expression, and reluctantly proceeded to open the safe. He tried to shield the interior with his body, but Quincannon loomed up behind to watch the troll's hands as they sifted through the contents.

"If I find out you've withheld so much as a collar stay,"

Quincannon warned him, "I'll pay you a return visit that won't be half so pleasant as this one."

Duff sighed and brought forth a chamois pouch, which he handed over with even greater reluctance. Quincannon holstered the Navy, shook the contents of the pouch into his palm. One ruby-studded brooch, two pairs of ruby earrings, and a diamond stickpin.

"This is only a small portion of the Dodger's ill-gotten gains. Where's the rest?"

"I don't know. I swear this is all he brought me!"

"When was he here?"

"Yesterday morning. He said he had more, that he'd bring them in a day or two, but I haven't seen him since."

"How much did you pay for the privilege of fencing these baubles?"

"Two hundred dollars. He . . . ah . . . seemed to think they were worth more, but he took the cash. He seemed in a hurry."

"Yes? Frightened, was he?"

"No. Eager, excited about something. All in a lather."

"Did he give you an idea of what had raised his blood pressure?"

"None. He grabbed the cash and ran out."

Quincannon nodded. He returned the items of jewelry to the pouch, tucked the pouch into his coat pocket.

"Here, now!" the troll cried. "You can't . . . that's my property!"

"No, it isn't. Not yours and not Dodger Brown's. These sparklers belong to Judge Adam Winthrop, the Dodger's first burglary victim. Don't worry, I'll make sure they're returned to the judge safe and sound, with your compliments."

Duff looked as if he were about to burst into tears.

"*Gahh,*" he said.

XI

A trolley car delivered Quincannon to the Ferry Building at the foot of Market Street. Ferries for the East Bay left every twenty to thirty minutes, and he arrived just in time to catch one of the Southern Pacific boats. A chilly half hour later, he disembarked with the other passengers and made his way up the Estuary to the Oakland City Wharf.

The place was a mixture of the colorful and the squalid. Arctic whalers, Chinese junks, Greek fishing boats, Yankee sailing ships, disreputable freighters, scows, sloops, shrimpers, oyster boats, houseboats; long rows of warehouses crowded here and there by shacks fashioned from bits and pieces of wreckage or from dismantled ships; long, barren sandpits. He approached three men in turn to ask the whereabouts of an oysterman named Salty Jim, owner of a boat with Oyster in the name. The first two either didn't know or wouldn't say, but the third, a crusty old sailor with a tam-o'-shanter pulled down over his ears, who sat propped against an iron cleat with a half-mended fishnet across his lap, knew Salty Jim well enough. And clearly didn't like him. He screwed up his face and spat off the wharf side.

"Salty Jim O'Bannon," he said, "ain't no oyster man."

"No? What is he?"

"A damn' oyster pirate, that's what."

Involved in the oyster trade, indeed, Quincannon thought sardonically. He'd had a run-in with oyster pirates once and did not relish a repeat performance. They were a scurvy lot, the dregs of the coastal waters—worse by far than Chinese shrimp raiders or Greek salmon poachers. At the first flood tide in June, an entire fleet of them would head down the bay to Asparagus Island to set up raiding parties on the beds. And much of the harvest would be stolen despite the efforts of the Fish Patrol and private operatives such as Quincannon. The only thing that kept the pirates from taking complete control of the bay waters was their own viciousness. Regular consumption of alcohol and opium combined with meanness had led to many a cutting scrape and many a corpse in the sandpits.

"How come you're lookin' for the likes of Salty Jim O'Bannon?" the old man asked. "Not fixin' to join up with him, are you?"

"No chance of that. It's not him I'm after."

"Who, then?"

"A cousin of his, Dodger Brown. Know the lad?"

"Can't say I do. Don't want to, if he's as black-hearted as Salty Jim."

"He may be, at that."

"What's his dodge? Not another pirate, is he?"

"Housebreaker."

"And what're you? You've got the look and questions of a nabber."

"Policeman?" Quincannon was mildly offended. "Manhunter on the scent is more like it. Where does Salty Jim keep his boat? Hereabouts?"

"Hell. He wouldn't dare. He anchors off Davis Wharf. Don't tie up for fear of somebody stealin' on board at night and murderin' him in his sleep."

"What's her name?"

"*Oyster Catcher*. Now ain't that a laugh?"

"He lives on her, does he?"

"He does. Might find him there now, but you better be carryin' a pistol and not shy about usin' it."

Quincannon made his way to Davis Wharf. Several sloops and schooners were anchored in the bay nearby, so many that he wasted no time in trying to pick out the *Oyster Catcher*. A ragged youth who was fishing with a hand line off the wharf side made the identification for him; the youth also agreed to rent Quincannon his own patched skiff beached in the tidal mud fifty rods distant. Unlike the old fisherman, the boy seemed impressed that Quincannon was on his way to talk to Salty Jim, the oyster pirate; the shine of hero worship was in his eyes. Quincannon repressed the urge to shake some sense into him. You couldn't hope to make everyone walk the straight and narrow. Besides, a new generation of crooks meant continued prosperity for Carpenter and Quincannon, Professional Detective Services well into his and Sabina's dotage.

He stowed his grip in the skiff, rowed out to the *Oyster Catcher*. She was a good-size sloop with a small cabin amidships, her mainsail furled, her hull in need of paint but otherwise in good repair. No one was on deck, but from inside the cabin he could hear the discordant strumming of a banjo. He shipped his oars until he was able to draw in next to a disreputable rowboat tied to a portside Jacob's ladder. He tied the skiff's painter to another rung, drew his Navy, and climbed quickly on board.

The banjo player heard or felt his presence; the instrument twanged and went silent, and a moment later the cabin door burst open and a bear of a man, naked to the waist, stepped out with a belaying pin clenched in one hand. Quincannon snapped—"Stand fast!"—and brought the pistol to bear. The fellow pulled up short, blinking and scowling. He was thirtyish, sported a patchy beard and hair that hung in matted ropes. The cold bay wind blew the smells of Dr. Hall and body odor off him in such a ripe wave that Quincannon's nostrils pinched in self-defense.

"Who in foggy hell're you?"

"My name is of no matter to you. Drop your weapon."

"Huh?"

"The belaying pin. Drop it, Jim."

Salty Jim gaped at him, rubbing at his scraggly beard with his free hand, his mouth open at least two inches—a fair approximation of a drooling idiot. "What's the idee comin' on my boat? You ain't the gawd-damn' fish patrol."

"It's your cousin I want, not you."

"Cousin?"

"Dodger Brown. If he's here, call him out. If he's not, tell me where I can find him."

"I ain't gonna tell you nothin'."

"You will, or you'll find a lead pellet nestling in your hide."

The oyster pirate's mean little eyes narrowed to slits. He took a step forward and said with drunken belligerence: "By gar, nobody's gonna shoot me on my own boat."

"I'm warning you, Jim. Drop your weapon and hold still, or. . . ."

Salty Jim was too witless and too much taken with drink to be either scared or intimidated. He growled deeply in his throat, hoisted the belaying pin aloft, and mounted a lumbering charge.

Quincannon had no desire to commit mayhem if it could be avoided. He took two swift steps forward, jabbed the Navy's muzzle hard and straight into the pirate's sternum. Salty Jim said—"Uff!"—and rounded at the middle like an archer's bow. The blow took the force out of his downsweeping arm; the belaying pin caromed more or less harmlessly off the meaty part of Quincannon's shoulder. Another jab with the Colt, followed by a quick reverse flip of the weapon, a trick he'd learned from his father, and with the butt end a solid thump on the crown of the pirate's empty cranium. There was another satisfying *"Uff!,"* after which Salty Jim stretched out on the scaly deck for a nap. Rather amazingly he even commenced to make snoring noises.

Quincannon prodded him with the toe of his shoe; the nap and the snores continued unabated. He holstered the Navy and proceeded to frisk the man's never-washed trousers and shirt. This netted him nothing except a sack of Bull Durham, some papers, and a greasy French postcard of no artistic merit whatsoever.

He picked up the belaying pin, tossed it overboard. A frayed belt that held up the pirate's trousers served to tie his hands behind his back. Quincannon then stepped over the unconscious man, entered the cabin.

He had been in hobo jungles and opium dens that were tidier and less aromatic. Mouth breathing, he searched the confines. It was evident from the first that two men lived here recently. Verminous blankets were wadded on each of the two bunks, and there were empty bottles of the cheap and potent whiskey known as Dr. Hall, evidently Salty Jim's tipple, and empty bottles of the foot juice favored by Dodger Brown. The galley table, however, bore remnants of a single meal of oyster stew and sourdough bread, one tin coffee mug, one dirty glass, and one bottle of Dr. Hall.

Under one of the bunks was a pasteboard suitcase. Quincannon drew it out, laid it on the blankets, snapped the cheap lock with the blade of his pocket knife, and sifted through the contents. Cheap John clothing of a size much too small to fit Salty Jim. An oilskin pouch that contained an array of lock picks and other burglar tools. An old Smith & Wesson revolver wrapped in cloth, unloaded, no cartridges in evidence. And a larger, felt-lined cloth sack that rattled provocatively as he lifted it out. When he upended the sack onto the blanket, out tumbled a variety of jewelry, timepieces, small silver and gold gewgaws. Pay dirt! A quick accounting told him that he was now in possession of all the stolen goods from the first three robberies.

There was one other item of interest in the suitcase, which he'd missed on his first look. It lay on the bottom, face down, caught under a torn corner. He fished it out, flipped it over. A business card, creased and thumb-marked, but not of the sort he himself carried. He had seen such discreet advertisements before; they had grown more or less common in the Uptown Tenderloin, handed out by the more enterprising businesswomen in the district. This one read:

FIDDLE DEE DEE
Miss Lettie Carew Presents
Bountiful Beauties from Exotic Lands
Maison de Joie   244 O'Farrell Street

Well, well, Quincannon thought. *Is that why you were so eager for cash yesterday, you young scamp? And why you didn't spend last night on this scabrous tub?*

He considered. Should he wait here for the Dodger's return? Or should he chance that his quarry had not only elevated his taste in bawdy houses, but was still elevating? His instincts indicated the latter. His trust in them, and distaste at the prospect of a long vigil—perhaps a very long vigil—in the company of Salty Jim O'Bannon, made up his mind in short order.

He re-sacked and pocketed the swag, stepped out onto the deck with the Dodger's revolver in hand. Salty Jim was still *non compos,* but now starting to stir a bit. Quincannon left him bound, dropped the revolver into the bay, and further coppered his bet by untying and setting the rowboat adrift. Then, whistling "The Brewers Big Horses Can't Run Over Me", one of his favorite temperance songs, he climbed down into his rented craft and began to row briskly back to the wharf.

XII

The district known as the Uptown Tenderloin was a pocket of sin more genteel and circumspect than the Barbary Coast, catering to the more playful among the city's respectable citizens. It was located on the streets—Turk, Eddy, Ellis, O'Farrell—that slanted diagonally off Market. Some of San Francisco's better restaurants, saloons, and variety show theaters flourished here, part of the Cocktail Route that nightly drew the be-gowned and silk-hatted gentry. Smartly dressed young women paraded along Market during the evening hours, not a few of them wearing violets pinned to their jackets and bright-colored feather boas around their necks that announced them to those in the know as sporting ladies. Men of all ages lounged in front of cigar stores and saloons, engaged in a pastime that Quincannon himself had followed on occasion, known as "stacking the mash": ogling and flirting with parading ladies of both easy and well-guarded virtue.

Parlor houses also flourished here, so openly that the reform element had begun to mount a serious clean-up campaign. The most notorious was the one operated by Miss Bessie Hall, the "Queen of O'Farrell Street", all of whose girls were said to be blonde and possessed of rare talents in the practice of their trade. Lettie Carew and her Fiddle Dee Dee were among the second-rank of Bessie's rivals, specializing in ladies of other cultures and different hues.

The evening parade had yet to begin when Quincannon alighted from a Market Street trolley at O'Farrell Street, his pockets empty now of the stolen loot; he had stopped off at Carpenter and Quincannon, Professional Detective Services, and locked it away in the office safe. Above him, as he strolled along the wooden sidewalk, sundry flounced undergarments clung to telephone wires, another form of advertisement tossed out by the inhabitants of the shuttered houses along the route. This, too, had scandalized and provoked the reformers. Midway in the third block, he paused before a plain shuttered building that bore the numerals **244** on its front door. A small, discreet sign on the vestibule wall said **Fiddle Dee Dee** in gilt letters.

A smiling colored woman opened the door in answer to his ring and escorted him into an ornately furnished parlor, where he declined the offer of refreshment and requested an audience with Miss Lettie Carew. When he was alone, he sat on a red plush chair, closed his nostrils to a mingled scent of incense and patchouli, and glanced around the room with professional interest. Patterned lace curtains and red velvet drapes at the blinded windows. Several red plush chairs and settees, rococo tables, ruby-shaded lamps, gilt-framed mirrors, oil paintings of exotically voluptuous nudes. There were also a handful of framed mottoes, one of which Quincannon could read from where he sat: **If every man was as true to his country as he is to his wife . . . God help the U.S.A.** In all, the parlor was similar to Bessie Hall's, doubtless by design, although it was neither as lavish nor as stylish. None could match "the woman who licked John L. Sullivan" when it came to extravagance.

At the end of five minutes, Lettie Carew swept into the room. Quincannon blinked and managed not to let his jaw unhinge; Miss Lettie had been described to him on more than one occasion, but this was his first glimpse of her in the flesh. And a great deal of flesh there was. She resembled nothing so much as a giant cherub, pink and puffed and painted, dressed in pinkish white silk and trailing rose-hued feather boas and a cloud of sweet perfume that threatened to finish off what oxygen had been left undamaged by the patchouli and incense.

"Welcome, sir, welcome to Fiddle Dee Dee, home of many bountiful beauties from exotic lands. I am the proprietress, Miss Lettie Carew."

Quincannon blinked again. The madam's voice was small and shrill, not much louder than a mouse squeak. The fact that it emanated from such a mountainous woman made it all the more startling.

"What can I do for you, sir? Don't be shy . . . ask and ye shall receive. Every gentleman's pleasure is my command."

"How many Chinese girls are here?"

"Ah, you have a taste for the mysterious East. Only one . . . Ming Toy, from far-off Shanghai, and most popular she is, sir, most popular. Unfortunately she is engaged at present."

"How long has she been engaged?"

"I beg your pardon?"

"Since yesterday, perhaps? By the same man . . . young, slight, black-haired, whose tipple is red wine?"

Lettie Crew said suspiciously: "How did you know that?"

"Is he still here now?"

"Suppose he is. What's your interest in him?"

So he'd been right: the Dodger *was* still elevating. He managed not to smile. "Professional," he said. "The lad's a wanted felon."

The madam's subservient pose evaporated. "Oh, lordy, don't tell me you're a copper."

He didn't; he let her believe it from his stern expression.

"Bloody hell!" she said. "Can't you wait until he leaves before you arrest him? I have other customers upstairs. And I paid my graft this week, same as always. . . ."

"Which room is Ming Toy's?"

"There won't be shooting, will there?"

"Not if it can be avoided."

"If there's any damage, the city will pay for it or I'll sue. That includes bloodstains on the carpet, bedding, and furniture."

"What room, Lettie?"

She impaled him with a long smoky glare before she squeaked—"Nine."—and flounced out of the parlor.

In the hallway outside, a long carpeted staircase led to the second floor. Quincannon climbed it with his hand on the Navy Colt under his coat. The odd-numbered rooms were to the left of the stairs; in front of the door bearing a gilt-edged 9, he stopped to listen. No discernible sounds issued from within. He drew his revolver, depressed the latch, and stepped into a room decorated in an ostentatious Chinese dragon style, dimly lighted by rice-paper lanterns and choked with incense spiced with wine vapors.

An immediate skirmish, he was pleased to note, was unnecessary. Dodger Brown sprawled supine on the near side of the four-poster bed, dressed in a pair of soiled long johns, flatulent snoring sounds emanating from his open mouth. The girl who sat beside him was no more than twenty, delicate-featured, her comeliness marred by dark eyes already as old as Cain. She hopped off the bed, pulling a loose silk wrapper around her thin body, and hurried over to where Quincannon stood. If she noticed his drawn weapon, it made no apparent impression on her.

"Busy," she said in a singsong voice, "busy, busy."

"Not any more. It's him I'm after, not you."

"So?" The young-old eyes blinked several times. "Finished?"

"Finished," he agreed. "I'm taking him to jail."

She understood the word and it seemed to please her. She glanced at the snoring Dodger. "Wine," she said disgustedly.

"I'm a teetotaler myself."

Ming Toy wrinkled her nose. "Phooey," she said, and vanished as swiftly and silently as a wraith.

Quincannon padded to the bedside. Four rough shakes, and Dodger Brown stopped snoring and his eyes popped open. For several seconds he lay inert, peering up blearily at the face looming above him. Recognition came an instant before he levered himself off the bed in a single convulsive movement and lunged for the door.

On this occasion, however, Quincannon was ready for him and his sly tricks. He caught hold of the long john's collar with his free hand, spun the little burglar around, deftly avoided a shin kick, flung him backwards onto the rumpled bed, knelt beside him, and poked the bore of the Navy squarely between his bloodshot eyeballs. "Settle down, lad," he said. "You're yaffled this time and you know it."

The Dodger, staring cross-eyed at the Colt, knew it for a fact. All the struggle and sand left him at once; he lay in a motionless puddle, an expression of painful self-recrimination rearranging his vulpine features.

"It's my own fault," he said in mournful tones as Quincannon handcuffed him. "After you near snagged me the other night, I knew I should've hopped a rattler in the

Oakland yards straightaway. Gone on the lammas, 'stead of comin' over here."

"Aye, and let it be a lesson to you, Dodger." Quincannon grinned and added sagely: "The best-laid plans aren't always the best-planned lays."

XIII

The city prison, in the basement of the Hall of Justice, was a busy place that testified to the amount of crime afoot in San Francisco. And to Quincannon's practiced eye, there were just as many crooks on the outside of the foul-smelling cells as on the inside. Corrupt policemen, seedy lawyers haggling at the desk about releases for prisoners, rapacious fixers, deceitful bail bondsmen . . . more of those, in fact, than honest officers and men charged with felonies, and with vagrancy, public drunkenness, and other misdemeanors.

Quincannon delivered a sullen and uncommunicative Dodger Brown there, and spent the better part of an unpleasant hour talking to an officer he knew and a booking desk sergeant he didn't know. He signed a complaint on behalf of the Great Western Insurance Company and, before he left, made sure that the Dodger would remain locked in one of the cells until Jackson Pollard and Great Western Insurance officially formalized the charge. He knew better than to turn over any of the stolen goods, did not even mention that they were in his possession. Valuables had a curious way of disappearing from the police property room overnight.

By the time he reentered the offices of Carpenter and Quincannon, Professional Detective Services, it was late afternoon. He told Sabina of the day's events, embellishing a bit on his brief scuffles with Salty Jim and Dodger Brown.

"You take too many risks, John," she admonished him. "One of these days you'll pay dear for such recklessness. Just as your father and my husband did."

He waved that away. "I intend to die in bed at the age of ninety," he said. "And not alone, either."

"I wouldn't be surprised if either boast turned out to be true." Her mouth quirked slightly at the corners. "You had no difficulty finding your way around the Fiddle Dee Dee, I'm sure."

"Meaning what, my dear?"

"Don't tell me you've never been in a parlor house before."

"Only in the performance of my professional duty," he lied.

"If that's so, as randy as you are, I pity the fair maidens of San Francisco."

"I have no designs on the virtue of young virgins. Only on the favors of a certain young and handsome widow."

"Then you're fated to live out your years as celibate as a monk. Did Dodger Brown confess to his crimes?"

Quincannon sighed. Unrequited passion, especially when it was as pure as his for Sabina, was a sad and pitiable thing. "He had little to say after we left the Fiddle Dee Dee. A close-mouthed lad, the Dodger. But the loot from his burglaries will convict him."

"The Costain valuables weren't among the ones you recovered?"

"No," he said. "But I'll find them soon enough."

"There's still time to take the lot to Great Western and turn it over to Mister Pollard," Sabina said. "Shall I ring him up?"

"No. Best wait until the morrow."

"Why? Pollard came by earlier, all in a dither. Two more claims have taxed his patience to the limit."

"Two more?"

"Both filed today by Penelope Costain."

"One for the amount of her missing jewelry. The other?"

"The Costains also have a joint life insurance policy with Great Western. In the sum of twenty-five thousand dollars." Sabina's smile was wry. "The widow wasted little time."

"That she did."

"I managed to smooth Pollard's feathers, but the sooner he knows Dodger Brown is in custody and the loot has been recovered, the better for us. Do you expect to find the Costain valuables tonight? Is that why you want to wait?"

"It's one of the reasons," Quincannon said, although it wasn't.

"Another wouldn't concern Sherlock Holmes, would it?"

"What makes you think that?"

"I know you, John, much better than you think I do."

"Bosh," he said, and changed the subject. "What did you learn in your investigations today?"

By the time Sabina had finished her report, his freebooter's beard was split in a crooked smile. "Bully! Just as I suspected."

"Does that mean you've solved the puzzle?"

"It does. All I lack now are a few minor details."

"Well? How was Andrew Costain murdered? How was Dodger Brown able to escape from the house?"

"Not until tomorrow morning, my lady. Meet me at Pollard's office at nine-thirty. You'll hear the full explanation then."

"You're being exasperating again, John Quincannon.

Why can't you just give me the jist of it now?"

He said—"Nine-thirty, sharp."—teased her further with a fiendish wink, and took his leave.

On Market Street he hailed a cab. He hadn't eaten since breakfast and his hunger was fierce, but there was an important errand that needed doing first. He gave the hack driver Dr. Caleb Axminster's Russian Hill address.

Some thirty minutes later, an owl-eyed housekeeper opened the Axminsters' front door and informed him that the doctor had not yet returned from his surgery. From behind her, somewhere in the house, Quincannon could hear the cheerful, somewhat fantastic plucking of violin strings—no melody he had ever heard before. He said: "It's Mister Sherlock Holmes I've come to see," and handed the housekeeper one of his business cards. She took it away with her. Soon the violin grew silent, and, shortly after that, the housekeeper returned to take him to a sitting room off the main parlor.

Holmes was sprawled comfortably in an armchair, his violin now on a table beside him. In his lap was a small bottle of clear liquid and a morocco case. He greeted Quincannon, asked him to wait a moment. With long, nervous fingers he then produced a hypodermic syringe from the case, filled it from the bottle, adjusted the needle, and rolled up his left shirt cuff. On the sinewy forearm and wrist Quincannon spied innumerable puncture marks. As he watched, Holmes thrust the needle into his arm, pressed the plunger, and then sank back with a long sigh of satisfaction.

"What's in the bottle, Holmes?"

The Englishman smiled. "A seven-percent solution," he said, "courtesy of the good Doctor Axminster."

Quincannon did not have to ask the exact nature of the

seven-percent solution. He shrugged and let the matter drop. Each man to his own vice.

"Well, my esteemed colleague," Holmes said, "I must say I'm glad you've come. I intended to call on you earlier, but I've had rather a busy day. You have saved me the necessity of going out again this evening."

"I've had a busy day myself. And a highly productive one."

"You've located Dodger Brown?"

"Located and arrested him. And recovered the burglary loot."

"My dear Quincannon, you surpass yourself!"

"That news is not the only reason for my visit," Quincannon said silkily. "I've also brought you an invitation."

"Invitation?"

"To a meeting in the offices of Jackson Pollard, head of the claims department for the Great Western Insurance Company, at nine-thirty tomorrow morning. If you'll consent to attend, I'll guarantee you'll find it edifying."

"In what regard?"

"I intend to explain the mystery surrounding the death of Andrew Costain."

"Ah! So your sleuthing has reaped additional rewards, has it?"

"It has."

"And now there is to be a public unveiling," Holmes said. "Splendid. You and I are more alike than either of us might care to admit, Quincannon. Often enough a touch of the artist wells up in me, too, and calls insistently for a well-staged performance."

"Then you'll be there?"

"Oh, by all means." Holmes's eyes were bright; he

seemed not at all nonplussed to have been outdone. "I shall be most interested to hear your deductions. Most interested, indeed!"

XIV

The San Francisco offices of Great Western Insurance were housed in the Montgomery Block, the largest of the city's buildings at Montgomery and Merchant streets. It was just nine-thirty of another cold, gloomy morning when Quincannon entered the anteroom. He found Sabina and Sherlock Holmes already present, along with two other principals he hadn't expected to see—Penelope Costain and Dr. Caleb Axminster. Holmes had invited both of them, it turned out, because Mrs. Costain had a vested concern in the proceedings and Axminster was an interested party. Quincannon had no objection in either case. If he hadn't been so involved in his competition with Holmes, he would have thought of it himself.

In a body they were shown into Jackson Pollard's private sanctum. The claims adjustor was a fussy, bespectacled little man with sparse sandy hair and sideburns like miniature tumbleweeds. He demanded, frowning: "What's the meaning of this, Quincannon? Why are all these people here?"

"As witnesses, you might say."

"Witnesses to what?"

"That will soon become evident. Will you have chairs brought in to accommodate everyone?"

This was done, and all sat down except Quincannon. Holmes lit his oily clay pipe and sat in a relaxed posture, a small smile playing at the corners of his mouth. Sabina sat quietly with hands clasped in her lap; patience was one of her many virtues. Penelope Costain was less at ease, fidgeting in her chair, fingers toying with a tiger-eye and agate locket at her throat. Axminster sucked on hoarhound drops, wearing the bright-eyed, expectant look of a small boy on Christmas morning.

Pollard said: "Well, Quincannon? Get on with it." He had no patience at all. "And what you have to say had better be to my liking."

"It will be," Quincannon assured him. "First of all, Dodger Brown is in custody awaiting formal charges. I tracked him down and arrested him yesterday."

"Yesterday? Why didn't you notify me immediately?"

"I had my reasons."

"Yes? What about all the items he stole? Did you recover them?"

"I did."

Quincannon had stopped by the agency offices on his way here; he drew out the sack of valuables and, with a flourish, placed it on Pollard's desk blotter. The little man's eyes glowed pleasurably as he spread the contents out in front of him, but the glow faded a bit once he'd sifted through the lot. "All present and accounted for from the first three burglaries," he said. "But none of Missus Costain's losses is here."

"I haven't recovered those items as yet."

"But you do have an idea of what Brown did with them?"

"He did nothing with them. He never had them."

"Never had them, you say?"

"Dodger Brown didn't burgle the Costain home," Quincannon said. "Nor is he the murderer of Andrew Costain."

Pollard blinked owlishly behind his spectacles. "Then who did burgle it?"

"No one."

"Come, come, man, speak plainly, say what you mean."

"It was Andrew Costain who planned the theft, with the aid of an accomplice, and it was the accomplice who punctured him and made off with the contents of the valuables case."

This announcement brought forth an *"Ahh!"* from Dr. Axminster. Sabina arched one of her fine eyebrows. Even Sherlock Holmes sat up straight in his chair, his expression intent.

Penelope Costain said icily: "That is a ridiculous accusation. Why on earth would my husband conspire to rob his own home?"

"To defraud Great Western Insurance Company. In order to pay off his substantial gambling debts. Surely you know he was a compulsive gambler, Missus Costain. And that his finances had been severely depleted and his law practice had suffered setbacks as a result of his addiction."

"I knew no such thing."

"If it's true," Pollard said, "how did *you* find it out?"

"I was suspicious of him from the moment he asked me to stand watch on his property." This was not quite true, but what harm in a little embellishment? "Two nights ago at Doctor Axminster's, he seemed to consider me something of an incompetent buffoon for allowing Dodger Brown to escape at the Truesdale home. Why then would he choose me of all people to protect his property? The answer is that he *wanted* a detective he considered inept to bear witness to a cleverly staged break-in. Underestimating me was his first mistake."

"Was that the only thing that made you suspicious?"

"No. Costain admitted it was unlikely that a professional housebreaker, having had a close call the previous night, would risk another crime so soon, yet he would have me believe his fear was so great he was willing to pay dear for two operatives to stand surveillance on successive nights. An outlay of funds he could ill afford, for it was plain from his habitual drinking and the condition of his office that he had fallen on difficult times. He also made the dubious claim that he had no time to remove valuables from his home and secret them elsewhere until Dodger Brown was apprehended, and no desire to cancel 'important engagements' in order to guard his premises himself."

Axminster asked: "So you accepted the job in order to find out what he was up to?"

"Yes." Another embellishment. He had accepted it for the money—no fool, John Quincannon. "Subsequent investigations by Missus Carpenter"—he bowed to Sabina—"revealed Costain's gambling addiction and a string of debts as long as a widowed mother's clothesline. He was a desperate man."

"You suspected insurance fraud, then," Holmes said, "when you asked me to join you in the surveillance."

"I did," Quincannon lied.

"Did you also suspect the manner in which the fraud would be perpetrated?"

"The use of an accomplice dressed in the same type of dark clothing as worn by Dodger Brown? Costain's arrival not more than a minute after the intruder entered the house through the rear door? Not until later. It was a devious plan that no detective could have anticipated in its entirety before the fact. In truth, a bughouse caper from start to finish."

"Bughouse caper?"

"Crazy scheme. Fool's game."

"Ah. Crook's argot, eh? More of your delightful American idiom."

Pollard said: "So the accomplice pulled a double-cross, is that it? He wanted the spoils all for himself?"

"Just so," Quincannon agreed.

"Name him."

"Not just yet. Other explanations are in order first."

"Such as how Costain was murdered in a locked room? And why he was shot as well as stabbed? Can you answer those questions?"

"I can," Quincannon said, not to Pollard but to Sherlock Holmes. The alleged world's greatest detective was about to lose his mantle to a more worthy rival, and Quincannon intended to savor every moment of his triumph.

"Well, then?"

Quincannon produced his pipe and tobacco pouch, allowing suspense to build while he loaded the bowl. Holmes watched him in a rapt way, his hands busy winding a pocket Petrarch, his expression neutral except for the faintest of smiles. The others, Sabina included, were on the edges of their chairs.

When he had the pipe lit and drawing well, he said: "The answer to your first question, Mister Pollard," he said to Holmes, "is that Andrew Costain was *not* murdered in a locked room. Nor was he stabbed *and* shot by his accomplice."

"Riddles, Quincannon?" Pollard said irritably.

"Not at all. To begin with, Andrew Costain shot himself." Quincannon paused for dramatic effect before continuing. "The report was designed to draw me into the house, the superficial wound to support what would have been his claim of a struggle with the thief. The better to bamboozle me, so he reasoned, and the better to insure that Great Western would pay off his claim quickly and without question or suspicion."

"How did you deduce the sham?"

"Dodger Brown was known to carry a pistol in the practice of his trade, but only for purposes of intimidation . . . he had no history of violence. I'll wager that he carried his weapon unloaded, for it was empty when I found it yesterday in his hide-out and there were no cartridges among his possessions. The revolver that inflicted the wound was bought new that same day in a gunsmith's shop near Costain's law offices, by Costain himself. Missus Carpenter's investigation revealed this information, and that concerning his financial troubles."

"But why the locked room business?" Sabina asked. "Further obfuscation?"

"No. In point of fact, there was no locked room ploy."

Pollard growled: "Dammit, Quincannon. . . ."

"That part of the misadventure was a mix of illusion and accident, the result of circumstances, not premeditation. There was no intent to gild the lily with such theatrics. Even if there had been, there was simply not enough time for any sort of locked room gimmick to have been perpetrated once the pistol was fired."

"Then what did transpire?"

"Costain was in the hallway outside the open door to his study, not inside the room, when he discharged the shot into his forearm. That is why the electric light was on in the hall . . . why the smell of burned powder was strong there, yet all but nonexistent inside the room. The bullet penetrated the armchair because the gun was aimed in that direction when it was fired, through the open doorway into the study."

"Why didn't Costain simply fire the shot in there?"

"I suspect he met his accomplice in the hallway, perhaps to hand over the jewelry from the valuables case. The empty case was another clue that put me onto the gaff. The time factor again . . . there was too little time for the phantom burglar to have found his way to the study, located the case, and rifled it before Costain arrived to catch him in the act."

"And the murder, John?" Sabina asked.

"Within moments of the shot being fired, the accomplice struck. Costain was standing in the open doorway, his back to the hallway. The force of the single stab with a long, narrow blade staggered him forward into the study. The blow was not immediately fatal, however. He lived long enough to turn, confront his attacker, observe the bloody weapon in a hand still upraised . . . and, in self-defense, to slam the door shut and twist the key already in the latch. Then he collapsed and died."

"Why didn't he shoot the accomplice instead?" Axminster said. "That is what I would have done."

"He may no longer have held the pistol. Either the suddenness of the attack caused him to drop it, or he dropped it in order to lock the door against his betrayer. In my judgment Andrew Costain was a craven coward as well as a thief. I think, if pressed, his wife would agree, despite her allegation to the city police that he was a brave man."

Penelope Costain's face was the shade of egg white. "I agree with nothing you've said. Nothing!"

Sherlock Holmes stirred in his chair. The grudging admiration in his eyes brought a warm glow to Quincannon. His gloat, however, was not to last long.

"Capital, Quincannon!" Holmes said. He bounced to his feet and grasped Quincannon's hand. "I congratulate you on your performance thus far. You've done a commendable job of interpreting the *res gestæ*."

"*Res* what?" Pollard asked.

"The facts of the case. My learned colleague's deductions coincide almost exactly with mine."

Quincannon stiffened. "What's that? *Your* deductions?"

"Oh, yes, certainly. I reached the identical conclusions yesterday afternoon."

"Hogwash!"

"My dear fellow, you doubt my word?"

"I do, unless you can name the accomplice and explain the rest of what took place."

"I can. Naturally."

Damn his eyes! "Well? Who stabbed Costain?"

"His wife, of course. Penelope Costain."

A startled noise came from Pollard. Mrs. Costain's only reaction was to lighten another shade and draw herself up indignantly. "I?" she said with chilly bluster. "How dare you!"

Quincannon said quickly: "Dodger Brown is a small man. It was easy enough for you to pass for him in the darkness, dressed in dark man's clothing, with a cloth cap covering your hair."

"Quite so," Holmes agreed. He relit his pipe before he continued. "While joined in her husband's plan, she devised a counter-plan of her own . . . her double-cross, as you Americans call it . . . for two reasons. First, to attempt to defraud the Great Western Insurance Company not once but twice, by entering claims on both the allegedly stolen jewelry and on her husband's twenty-five thousand dollar life insurance policy, of which she is the sole beneficiary. She came to this office yesterday to enter those claims, did she not, Mister Pollard?"

"She did."

"Her second motive," Holmes went on, "was hatred, a virulent and consuming hatred for the man to whom she was married."

"You can't possibly know that," Quincannon objected. "You're guessing."

"I do not make guesses. Missus Costain's hatred of her husband was apparent to me at Doctor Axminster's dinner party. My eyes have been trained to examine faces and not their trimmings . . . their public disguise, as it were. As for proof of her true feelings, and of her guilt, I discovered the first clue shortly after we found Andrew Costain's corpse."

"What clue?"

"Face powder," Holmes said.

"Eh? Face powder?"

"When I examined the wound in Andrew Costain's back through my glass, I discovered a tiny smear of the substance on the cloth of his cheviot . . . the same type and shade as worn by Missus Costain."

"How could that prove her guilt? They were married . . . her face powder might have gotten on his coat at any time, in a dozen different ways."

"I beg to differ. It was close and to the right of the wound, which indicated that the residue must have adhered to the murderer's hand when the fatal blow was struck. It was also caked and deeply imbedded in the fibers of the cloth. This fact, combined with the depth of the wound itself, further indicated that the blade was plunged into Costain's flesh with great force and fury. An act born of hatred as well as greed. The wound itself afforded additional proof. It had been made by a stiletto, hardly the type of weapon a professional panny-man such as Dodger Brown would carry. A stiletto, furthermore, as my researches into

97

crime have borne out, is much more a woman's weapon than a man's."

Quincannon sought a way to refute this logic, and found none. He glowered and held his tongue.

Penelope Costain once again protested outraged innocence. No one paid her any attention, least of all Quincannon and Holmes.

"Now then," Holmes continued, "we have the mystery of Missus Costain's actions after striking the death blow. Her evidently miraculous escape from the house, only to reappear later dressed in evening clothes. Of course you know how this bit of flummery was managed, Quincannon."

Quincannon hesitated. Hell and damn! This was the one point about which he was not absolutely certain.

"Of course," he said.

"Pray elaborate."

He drew a breath and plunged ahead authoritatively. "There is little enough mystery in what she did. She simply hid until you and I were both inside the study and then slipped out. Through one of the windows, no doubt. She could easily have prepared one in advance so that it slid up and down noiselessly, and also loosened its latch just enough to allow it to drop back into the locking slot after she climbed through and lowered the sash. The window would then appear to be unbreached."

"Ingenious."

"She may have thought so."

"I meant your interpretation," Holmes said. "Unfortunately, however, you are wrong. That is not what she did."

"The devil you say!"

"Quite wrong on all counts except that she did, in fact, hide for a length of time. She could not have foreseen that both front and rear doors would be blocked so as to impede egress . . . if simple escape had been the plan, she could reasonably have expected to slip out one or the other door, thus obviating use of a window. Nor could she be certain in advance that a loosened window latch would drop back into its slot and thus go unnoticed. Nor could she be certain that we would fail to hear her raising and lowering the sash, and capture her before she could flee."

Quincannon said: "I suppose you have a better theory?"

"Not a theory . . . the exact truth of the matter. Her hiding place was the very same one she and her husband had decided upon as part of the original scheme. I confirmed it yesterday afternoon, when I returned to the Costain home while Missus Costain was here with Mister Pollard and spent two hours in an exhaustive search of the premises."

"You illegally entered my home?" This time, Penelope Costain's outrage was not feigned. "I'll have you arrested for trespassing!"

"I think not. Under the circumstances, I'm sure even the police would consider my actions fully justified. Doctor Axminster accompanied me, incidentally, at my request. He will confirm all that I am about to reveal."

"Indeed, I will," the doctor said.

Quincannon asked testily: "Then how *did* she escape from the blasted house?"

"She didn't. She never left it." Holmes paused as Quincannon had done earlier, for dramatic effect. "When you have eliminated the impossible," he said, "whatever is left must, perforce, be the truth. As applied in this case, I concluded as you did that it was impossible for Andrew Costain's slayer to have committed murder in and then escaped from the locked study . . . therefore Costain could not have been slain inside the study, and the study could not have been locked when the stiletto was plunged into his body. I concluded further that it was impossible for the slayer to have escaped the locked house after commission of the crime . . . therefore, she did not escape from it. Penelope Costain was hidden on the premises the entire time."

"Where? We searched the house from top to bottom."

"Indeed. But consider this . . . two strangers cannot possibly know every nook and cranny of a home in which they have never before set foot. The owners, on the other hand, are fully intimate with every detail of the premises."

A flush began to creep out of Quincannon's now rather tight collar. The light of knowledge had begun to dawn in the nooks and crannies of his nimble brain. He cursed himself for his failure to see what the bloody Englishman had seen much sooner.

"During my search this afternoon," Holmes continued, "I discovered a small adjunct to the kitchen pantry . . . a tiny room where preserves and the like are stored. The entrance to the room is concealed behind a pantry shelf. Those who knew of it could be reasonably sure that the entrance would be overlooked by strangers. The room itself is some four feet square, and, while it has no ventilation, its door when cracked open permits normal breathing. Missus Costain had no trouble remaining hidden there for well over an hour . . . ample time for her to change from the dark man's clothing into evening clothes she had secreted there earlier. After the arrival of the city police, when none of the officers was in the immediate vicinity, she slipped out through the kitchen and dining room to the front hallway and pretended to have just arrived home. The first person to encounter her, Sergeant Mahoney, had no reason to doubt this."

"But you did, I suppose."

"Oh, quite. When she first entered the study, I observed the remnants of cobwebs and traces of dust on the hem of her skirt, the fur of her wrap, even the ostrich plume in her hat. The pantry room contains cobwebs, dust, and dirt of the same type. I also observed that a piece had been torn from one of her fingernails, leaving a tiny wound in the cuticle. Earlier, during my studies of the carpet in the hallway, I discovered that same tiny piece, stained with a spot of fresh blood . . . broken off, of course, when she stabbed her husband. *Quod erat demonstrandum.*"

Penelope Costain said: "You can't prove any of this."

"Ah, but I can," Holmes told her. "After I left your home yesterday, I visited city police headquarters and spoke to Sergeant Mahoney and one of the officers who were stationed outside your home on that fateful night. Both swore an oath that no conveyance arrived and no one entered the house through either the front or rear door. The inescapable conclusion is that you were concealed inside the entire time. As for the missing jewelry and coins, and the murder weapon. . . ." He produced a cloth from his coat pocket, which he proceeded to unfold on Pollard's desk. Inside was a bloodstained stiletto and the stolen valuables. "As you see, Missus Costain, they are no longer where you hid them in the pantry room."

Both her icy calm and her bluster vanished at once; she sagged in her chair, lowered her head into her hands.

The others, Quincannon excepted, gazed at Holmes with open admiration. Even Sabina seemed more impressed by his performance than that of her doting partner. Holmes placed his hand over his heart and bowed as if responding to applause—a damned theatrical gesture if ever there was one. Then he faced Quincannon again, smiling indulgently.

"Have you any other questions, my good fellow?" he asked.

Questions? Quincannon had a brace of them, as a matter of fact. One: how soon will you be leaving San Francisco? Two: will I be able to stop myself from strangling, bludgeoning, stabbing, or shooting you before you do?

XV

"The man is infuriating!" Quincannon ranted. "Insufferable, insulting, exasperating!"

"John, for heaven's sake. . . ."

"Thinks he's a blasted oracle. Sees all, knows all. He's an expert on every arcane subject under the sun. He's full of. . . ."

"John."

". . . hot air. Enough to fill a balloon and carry it from here to the Sandwich Islands. Rattlepate! Braggart! Conceited popinjay!"

"Lower your voice," Sabina said warningly. "The other diners are starting to stare at us."

Quincannon subsided. She was right. The Cobweb Palace, Abe Warner's eccentric eatery on Meiggs Wharf in North Beach, was a noisily convivial place at the dinner hour, and to draw attention here required a considerable amount of bombast. The ramshackle building was packed to its creaking rafters on this evening—with customers partaking of the finest seafood fare in the city, and with the usual complement of monkeys, roaming cats and dogs, and such exotic birds as the parrot that was capable of hurling curses in four languages. Warner had a benevolent passion for all creatures large and small, including spiders; his collection of rare and sundry souvenirs, everything from Eskimo artifacts to a complete set of dentures that had once belonged to a sperm whale to rude paintings of nude women, were draped floor to ceiling in an undisturbed mosaic of cobwebs.

At length Sabina ventured to say: "I don't know why you carry on so much about Mister Holmes. He may be a bit full of himself, but there's no gainsaying the fact that he has a brilliant mind. Frankly I find him charming."

"Charming! You haven't spent nearly as much time with him as I have. Today's trek through the Barbary Coast and Chinatown was interminable. He insisted on seeing every squalid nook and cranny. Opium dens, gambling hells, wine dumps, half the pestholes from Dupont Street to the waterfront . . . yes, and the Hotel Nymphomania and Belle Cora's, among other parlor houses. He even stopped half a dozen street prostitutes to ask the prices for their services, not only for comparison here but with streetwalkers in London's Limehouse. *Faugh!* I had half a mind to bribe Ezra Bluefield to feed him a mickey finn and turn him over to the shanghaiers. . . ."

"Hush, now! That's enough."

Quincannon subsided again. He gave his attention to his abalone supper, attacking the succulent shellfish with a vengeance. Neither the attack nor his silence lasted for long, however. He laid his fork down after half a dozen bites. Gall had diminished his appetite; his stomach burned with dyspepsia. And now gloom was creeping in to dull the edge of his indignation.

He said: "That doctor friend of Holmes's in England,

what's-his-name, the one who sensationalizes all of his adventures . . . ?"

"Watson. And I wouldn't be too sure that he's a sensationalist."

"Bah. I suppose he'll write up this bughouse caper, too. And give Holmes all the credit for solving it. Omit my name entirely."

"I rather doubt it," Sabina said. "Holmes won't want it widely known that he was sleuthing in San Francisco or anywhere else during the past three years. Doctor Watson and the world at large have been led to believe he was dead, remember."

"A pity they're not right," Quincannon muttered.

"Really, John. I don't see why you're so jealous of the man."

"Jealous? Because he managed to solve part of the Costain case? I solved most of it myself, and found and arrested Dodger Brown and recovered the swag from his burglaries unto the bargain. I am every bit Holmes's equal, if not his better."

"Just as you say." Sabina sipped her glass of French wine. "It's not inconceivable, you know, that you'll have a biographer yourself someday."

Quincannon considered that statement. "I should have one now," he said. "By Godfrey, I should! I wonder if the gent who writes that pungent column for the *Examiner* would be interested."

"You mean Mister Ambrose Bierce?"

"That's the lad. Maybe I'll approach him about it."

"Well, his column *is* called 'Prattle'."

Quincannon ignored that. His gloom had begun to lift. "You're quite right, my lady, that I have no good cause to let that English pretender bother me. Sherlock Holmes . . .

hah! He may have achieved a small measure of fame, but fame is fickle and fleeting. In a few years his exploits will be forgotten. But the name and the detections of John Quincannon . . . ah, they're bound to be writ large and indelible in the annals of crime!"

Sabina rolled her eyes and remained eloquently silent.

The Cloud Cracker

The old watchman's shack was at the south end of the Delford railroad yards, a short walk from the station. Quincannon spied it as soon as he stepped down from the Stockton train. It was a ramshackle affair, listing a few degrees farther south on one side, its dusty windows blinded by squares of monk's cloth. Half a dozen citizens lounged in the shade of a row of locust trees nearby—far fewer, no doubt, than had been in attendance when the man calling himself Leonide Zacks began his rain-conjuring experiments five days ago.

The length of brand-new stovepipe that poked up more than a dozen feet through the shack's roof, and the streams of yellowish gas pouring from the pipe, gave the structure the look of a weirdly distorted steam boiler. An actual steam boiler was hidden from curious eyes inside—one of the items that made up Zacks's "miracle cloud-cracking machine". Among the others were a variety of chemicals, coils of copper tubing, a galvanic battery, and two large earthenware crocks. The crocks, Quincannon thought wryly, ought to have been given names: lightning mug for one, thunder mug for the other.

Alongside the shack stood a newly constructed platform, on top of which sat another odd contraption—a cross between a small-caliber cannon and a gigantic slingshot. It was in fact a kind of mortar whose alleged purpose was to assault the heavens with rockets containing a "secret chemical gas". Stretched between the platform and the building was a silken banner festooned with ribbons that hung limply in the hot dry air. Even from a distance Quincannon could read the crimson words emblazoned on the banner:

LEONIDE ZACKS
"THE CLOUD CRACKER"
**Peerless Drought Breaking
by the King of Pluviculturists
Results Guaranteed**

Not a trace of a cloud, cracked or otherwise, marred the smoky blue of the sky overhead. Quincannon would have been amazed if there had been. He would have been even more amazed to have smelled rain among the sharp odors of summer dust, river water, and the noxious perfume of the chemical gas. The heat here in the Central Valley was intense. Sweat slicked his forehead, trickled through the hairs in his gray-flecked freebooter's beard as he turned to peer in the opposite direction.

The town of Delford stretched out there, some five square blocks of it, its main street defined by orderly rows of gaslight standards—electricity hadn't yet come into general use here—and zinc-sheathed telegraph poles. There was not much activity, owing to the heat and the fact that this was a farm community still caught in the vise of a lengthy drought. Wheat fields surrounded it, broken only by the Southern Pacific tracks on one side and the San Joaquin River on the other.

"Mister Quincannon."

He swung toward the open doors to the station. One of his clients, Aram Kasabian, had appeared there and was hurrying toward him. Fiftyish, portly, wearing muttonchop whiskers and a black cheviot suit, Kasabian looked exactly like the prosperous small town banker he was. He had been on edge in San Francisco last week; today he appeared worried to the point of twitchiness.

"Well, Mister Kasabian. Good of you to meet me."

"I wanted to see you right away. I must say I'm relieved that you're here."

"Difficulties with Zacks and the Coalition?"

"Zacks and O.H. Goodland."

O.H. Goodland was Quincannon's other Delford client. He was one of the larger wheat farmers in the area and, based on their meeting in San Francisco, something of a narrow-minded hothead. Upon learning that the other half of Carpenter and Quincannon, Professional Detective Services, was a former female operative of the Pinkerton Agency's Denver office, Goodland had made disparaging remarks that earned him Quincannon's dislike. Men who saw no purpose to a woman other than cook and bed partner were horses' hindquarters.

"What's happened?" he asked the banker.

"O.H. threatened to kill Zacks last evening."

"Did he now. For what reason?"

"Evidently Zacks made improper advances to his daughter. Perhaps even seduced her. Molly denied the seduction, but O.H. isn't convinced."

Quincannon felt no surprise at this turn of events. The rainmaker had a reputation as a womanizer. "When were the advances made?"

"While O.H. and I were in San Francisco. He found out yesterday afternoon, when he came upon Molly crying in her room."

"The girl is smitten with Zacks?"

"It seems she was, before the advances."

"Does Missus Zacks know about this?"

"She wasn't present when O.H. accosted her husband, but I don't see how she could fail to have heard. Zacks's assistant, Collard, was there and it was in public, outside the Valley House."

"Accosted? Were blows struck?"

"Worse than that." Kasabian mopped his forehead with a silk handkerchief. "O.H. was carrying his revolver and he drew the weapon when Zacks gave him no satisfaction. Tom McCool disarmed him . . . he's our town marshal, if you remember . . . and warned against any further violence. But O.H. is stubborn, and a grudge holder . . . there's no telling what he might do."

"Is he back in town today?"

"He never left town," Kasabian said. "Took a room last night at the hotel, down the hall from Zacks's room. He's in the hotel saloon this very minute."

"Building his courage with whiskey?"

"Yes. O.H. is temperamental enough when he's sober, but under the influence he is twice as unpredictable."

This information made Quincannon scowl. He had no use for men who sought to solve their troubles with the aid of strong drink, having been such a man himself not so long ago. Toward the end of his fourteen-year stint as a U.S. Treasury operative he had accidentally shot and killed an innocent bystander during a gunfight, and this had led him into a prolonged period of drunkenness. Now, thanks in no small part to Sabina Carpenter, he was an ex-drunkard and a better fly cop than he'd been a government agent.

He said: "Leave Mister Goodland to me. Has there been any other trouble?"

"No, thank heaven."

"How is the Coalition taking Zacks's failure to bring rain?"

"There has been some grumbling, but he's a slick-tongued devil. Most of the people still have faith in him. He and Collard fired those chemical bombshells of theirs the last two nights and plan to do the same twice more. That's all it will take, he says. He promises at least one-half inch of rain by Monday morning or he'll return the advance payment."

"Which means," Quincannon said, "that unless a natural storm appears, he intends to vanish with the money by Sunday night. He won't, however. He'll be behind bars long before then."

Kasabian brightened. "He will? Missus Carpenter's wire said you were bringing good news. . . ."

"I'll share it after we've collected Mister Goodland."

Quincannon allowed the banker to pick up his carpetbag, lead the way through the station and north along Main. The heat lay heavy on his neck; that and O.H. Goodland's activities had tempered his good humor somewhat. He preferred San Francisco, with its cool fogs, and clients who acted in a reasonable fashion, thus permitting him to finish the task he had been hired to do and to take proper credit for it.

He and Sabina had accomplished this job swiftly. And he intended to be back in the city no later than Friday, two days from now, with the balance of their fee and a full compliment of satisfaction and good will. Leonide Zacks was a ruthless confidence man; bringing him to justice would be a feather in the caps of Carpenter and Quincannon, as well as save the Delford Coalition, a group of wheat farmers and merchants who had suffered hardest under the long drought, the $3,000 they had already paid to have rain clouds collected and cracked. But the feather wouldn't be half as tall if Zacks were shot dead by an irate father.

The collecting and cracking of Leonide Zacks would be
done tomorrow, legally and according to Quincannon's arrangements—a fact he meant to impress on O.H.
Goodland. With the barrel of his Navy Colt, if necessary.

The Valley House was a plain, two-story building opposite the bank. It had two entrances, one marked **Hotel** and
the other **Gentlemen's Saloon**. When he followed
Kasabian through the latter, Quincannon found himself in a
dim, stuffy room ripe with the smell of beer and spirits. He
wrinkled his nose, scanning the handful of patrons. O.H.
Goodland was not among them.

Kasabian was asking the barman where Goodland had
gone when loud, angry voices rose from the adjacent hotel
lobby. One, a tolerable bellow, Quincannon recognized as
the farmer's. He hurried through the archway separating
the saloon from the lobby.

At the foot of the staircase to the upper floor, Goodland
stood nose to nose with a slender young man in a cutaway
coat and brocade vest. A fair-haired woman dressed in
shirtwaist and Balmoral skirt was making an effort to push
Goodland away. He took no notice; she might have been
pushing at a rooted tree.

". . . all of you out of town before noon tomorrow," the
burly farmer was shouting, "or you'll suffer the consequences!" The words carried a faint whiskey slur. Veins
stood out on his thick neck; his face was the color of egg-
plant. "Hear me, Collard? By noon tomorrow!"

Ben Collard, Leonide Zacks's alleged assistant, was four
inches shorter and fifty pounds lighter, but he, too, stood
his ground. Flashing eyes and the hard set of his mouth be-
lied the dandified appearance given him by a curled mustache and sleekly pomaded hair. He was neither afraid of

Goodland nor intimidated by him.

"Your threats are worthless," he said. "We'll stay until we've fulfilled our contract to bring rain. . . ."

"Rain! Not a cloud much less a cloudburst in five days."

"We are scientists, not wizards."

Goodland uttered a rude word that brought a gasp from the woman. Quincannon thought the gasp was theatrical; Nora Zacks had likely heard—and spoken—far worse in her twenty-eight years. She was small and soft-looking, but there was sand and steel at the core of her.

She said with spirit: "You are vulgar, sir, as well as a drunkard and a fool."

"Better a vulgar fool than a charlatan and a debaucher."

"My husband did not seduce your daughter."

"You can't deny he made advances to her."

"I can and I do. Now will you kindly allow us to proceed to our rooms?"

"Proceed to the devil, the lot of you. You'll be welcomed with open arms."

At this insult Collard's control deserted him. He launched a blow without warning, one that had a good deal of force when it landed on the farmer's chin. Goodland reeled backward and went down, but only for the time it took him to shake his head and roar out an oath, then he scrambled to his feet with fists cocked. He would have charged the smaller man if Quincannon hadn't caught both his arms from behind, pinned them at his sides.

Goodland struggled, and, when he couldn't break loose, he swiveled his head to see who had him in such an iron grip. "Who in the name of . . . oh, it's you, Quincannon. Let me go."

"Not until you agree to behave."

"That damned fop hit me. . . ."

113

"You gave him a good reason."

Goodland repeated the rude word, tried again to pull free.

"You've had too much to drink and it's an infernally hot day. A bad combination, Mister Goodland." Quincannon applied pressure on the man's right arm, until Goodland grunted with pain and subsided. "Will you behave now?"

"All right, blast you. You needn't break my arm."

Quincannon shoved him to a nearby wing chair and bent him into it, none too gently. The farmer stayed put, massaging his arm and muttering to himself.

Nora Zacks said: "You have our gratitude, Mister . . . Quincannon, is it?"

He bowed. "John Quincannon, at your service."

She introduced herself and Collard. "I don't believe I've seen you in Delford before today."

"Mister Quincannon is from San Francisco," Kasabian said.

"A reporter with the *Call-Bulletin*," Quincannon lied glibly, "come to witness the marvels of pluviculture first-hand. I had hoped to arrive earlier in the week, but another matter kept me in the city. I seem not to have missed either a deluge or a sprinkle, so far."

"You may well see the latter before morning," Collard said.

"Indeed? And the former?"

"By the first of next week. Given enough time, the cloud cracker's miracle formula always produces the desired results."

"I look forward to meeting the great man."

"He'll want to meet you, too," Nora Zacks said. "Come to the rail yards before seven this evening and Mister Collard or I will introduce you."

"He'll be bruising the sky again with his rockets?"

"Yes. Promptly at seven."

When she and Collard had gone upstairs, Quincannon wasted no time in hoisting O.H. Goodland out of the wing chair, then marching him past a wide-eyed desk clerk and out through the hotel's rear door. The farmer's protests were mild; heat, exertion, and alcohol had combined to make him sluggish. Kasabian tagged along behind.

In the shade of the hotel livery barn Quincannon sat him down again on a bale of hay. A water pump and trough beckoned nearby. He pumped half a dipperful and then unceremoniously doused the farmer's head with it. This roused Goodland, brought him sputtering to his feet.

"How dare you! You . . . you. . . ."

"Are you sober enough now to listen to reason?"

"Mister Quincannon has news for us, O.H.," Kasabian told him hastily. "Good news about Zacks."

"That rascal's death is the only news that would cheer me." Goodland dried his face with the sleeve of his shirt. His spurt of anger seemed to dry with it. He regarded Quincannon with eyes that were bleary but focused. "Well! What's this news of yours?"

"Andrew Beadle."

"Beadle? You mean the county sheriff?"

"I do. He'll be arriving on the noon train from Fresno tomorrow. With two deputies and a warrant for the arrest of Cora and Leo Saxe and Harry Pollard."

"Saxe? Pollard?"

"The real names of the cloud cracker and his cohorts."

"They're wanted criminals, then?" Kasabian asked.

"In four Midwestern states."

"For what crimes?"

"The two men for confidence swindles back ten years, to

115

their days as theatrical performers in Chicago."

"Theatrical performers?"

"Low comedy and specialty acts in variety beer halls. More confidence men than you might think have such backgrounds. Since becoming professional swindlers they've left a trail of victims in Illinois, Ohio, Kansas, and Nebraska. Rainmaking is their most recent dodge, begun when Zacks married Cora Johnson in Omaha two years ago. Before that they posed as mining stock speculators, purveyors of a fountain-of-youth elixir, and inventors of an electric cancer cure."

"Frauds and highbinders," Goodland said. "By God, I knew it all along."

Kasabian asked: "How on earth did you find out so quickly, Mister Quincannon?"

The truthful answer was that he and Sabina had sent wires to other detective agencies across the country, providing specific information on the three rainmakers and their methods. The Pinkerton Agency's Chicago branch had been the most helpful. One of their operatives had developed a fascination with fraudulent pluviculturists after the debunking of the "Australian Rain Wizard", Frank Melbourne, who had achieved widespread publicity by allegedly "squeezing rain from cloudless skies as one would squeeze water from a sponge" in Ohio and Wyoming in 1891.

Melbourne had so thrived at first that other opportunists began claiming to have fantastic chemical or electrical machines and formulas of their own. Some, such as Clayton B. Jewell and the Kansas-based Inter State Artificial Rain Company, were quasi-legitimate exploiters who utilized Melbourne's trick of consulting long-range almanac forecasts and then gambling on a "no rain, no pay" basis. The out-and-out fleecers such as the cloud cracker worked only in communities where they were able to inveigle drought-weary citizens to pay half their exorbitant fees up front. If no natural storms arrived, allowing them to collect the balance, they were content to disappear with the half already paid.

Miffed as he was at O.H. Goodland, Quincannon was not inclined to tell the simple truth. He answered Kasabian's question by saying: "Detective work of the most advanced and perspicacious sort. Did you think you'd hired a commonplace agency when you came to us?"

"No, no, not at all. . . ."

Quincannon turned to the farmer. "Do you still consider me a fool for having a woman as my partner?"

"I never said you were a fool. I merely said it seemed a misguided choice."

"Misguided. Bah." Quincannon fixed him with a steely eye. "I trust you won't make a misguided choice, Mister Goodland."

"What do you mean by that?"

"Taking the law into your own hands."

"Put your mind at rest, Quincannon. Now that I know Zacks or Saxe or whatever the scoundrel's name is headed for prison, I'll not try to avenge my daughter's honor."

"You'll return to your farm, then?"

"No, that I won't do. Not until I see him arrested with my own eyes." Goodland paused, frowning, as a thought struck him belatedly. "Why aren't Beadle and his deputies already here to do their duty? Why are they waiting until tomorrow?"

"They have more urgent business in Fresno."

Goodland said—"More urgent business."—in disgusted tones. He added his favorite rude word and stalked away to the hotel.

★ ★ ★ ★ ★

Town marshal Tom McCool was a middle-aged, lantern-jawed man whose peacekeeping duties were mostly limited to the arrest of drunks and rowdies on Saturday night. Stolid and unimaginative, he had staunchly supported the Delford Coalition—the reason Kasabian and Goodland had bypassed him in their determination to expose the cloud cracker and gone to Carpenter and Quincannon instead.

Now, however, with matters coming to a head, it was necessary to enlist McCool's aid. Quincannon took Kasabian with him to the marshal's office, where he showed McCool wires from the Chicago Pinkertons and Sheriff Beadle as proof of the rainmakers' criminal backgrounds and imminent arrest. McCool offered no argument. He'd "grown some leery" of Zacks, he said, and also been worried over O.H. Goodland's lack of good sense. He promised to keep a sharp eye on the farmer and the three swindlers.

When Quincannon returned alone to the Valley House, to claim a room Kasabian had arranged for him, the desk clerk handed him a Western Union telegram that had just been delivered. It was from Fresno and it read:

ARRIVAL DELAYED UNTIL SIX PM TOMORROW
EARLIEST STOP REGRET ADDITIONAL DELAY
POSSIBLE WILL NOTIFY ASAP IN THAT EVENT

A BEADLE

"Hell and damn!" Quincannon said explosively, startling the clerk.

He read the wire again. "Regret additional delay possible" might mean Friday or even Saturday before Beadle and his deputies finally showed up in Delford. The prospect scratched at his temper like a thorn. The longer the delay, the shorter the odds that Goodland would lose his head or that Zacks would attempt to abscond with the Coalition's $3,000. The only sure way to avoid either of those occurrences was for him and McCool to make a citizens' arrest of the four individuals, and he was hesitant to do that except as a last resort. The legalities were tricky without the proper warrants.

There was another reason the delay troubled him. If he wasn't back in San Francisco by early Saturday morning, his and Sabina's plans for the weekend would have to be canceled. And important plans they were, confound it. . . .

He went from the hotel to the telegraph office and sent a wire to Sabina.

BEADLE DELAYED STOP RETURN SF BY SATURDAY MORNING IN JEOPARDY STOP IF MUST CANCEL EXCURSION WILL SUFFER GRAVE PAIN AND HEARTBREAK

JQ

Grave pain and heartbreak, indeed, he thought as he handed message and coins to the telegraph agent. Sabina's adamant refusal to permit their relationship to go beyond the professional had been a source of misery and frustration to him for nearly two years now. She was a handsome, desirable widow, and, while simple seduction had been his motive at first, this had rapidly changed to deeper and more poignant feelings. Now . . . well, he was smitten and no denying it. John Quincannon, confirmed bachelor, man of the world, hard-headed survivor of numerous misadventures, mooning and pining like a lovesick boy.

It had taken him months to convince her to join him on

an overnight pleasure trip, and her reluctant agreement to spend the coming weekend at Muir Woods seemed a sure sign that her defenses were crumbling at last. They would have separate rooms at their lodging house, to be sure, but, if all went well, such sleeping arrangements *could* be modified. At the very least they would be together in intimate surroundings. If the excursion had to be canceled, Sabina might balk at rescheduling.

Quincannon was sitting in a wing chair in a corner of the hotel lobby, pretending to read a two-day old copy of the Stockton *Record*, when Nora Zacks came downstairs. She was alone; her husband was still at the watchman's shack, and Collard had left twenty minutes earlier. He watched her walk across the lobby and outside. On her way to supper, he judged, before joining the men for the rocket assault. He consulted his Hampden pocket watch; the time was a quarter of six.

He laid the paper aside, climbed the stairs to the second floor. He had learned from the desk clerk which rooms were occupied by the Zacks and by Ben Collard; he went to the Zacks' suite first. The door was locked, of course, but this presented little difficulty for a man of Quincannon's talents. The handy little tool he carried in his pocket gave him access in less than a minute.

A thorough search of luggage and furnishings turned up no hint of the Coalition's $3,000. Finding and confiscating the cash was one way of ensuring that the three humbuggers remained in Delford until Sheriff Beadle's arrival. But it was a small hope at best. Chances were the greenbacks rested in a money belt worn around the cloud cracker's waist.

Quincannon relocked the door, and then picked the

latch on the one adjacent. The money was not in Collard's room, either. But he did find one item of interest, in plain sight on the stand next to the bed: a timetable for Southern Pacific's Central Valley passenger trains, with notations written in ink at the top. The notations read: **Stockton Limited, Thursday, six p.m.**

The day and time puzzled him. This Thursday, tomorrow? It would seem so; it was highly unlikely that the trio intended to remain here another eight days. And yet, it also seemed unlikely that they would be planning to leave so soon, by train and in broad daylight.

Their usual pattern was to dismantle the mortar under cover of darkness, load it and the rest of their rainmaking apparatus into their converted Dougherty wagon abandoning only the steam boiler, which had been obtained locally—and then vanish in the middle of the night.

Did they propose to abandon everything this time? If so, why? And how did they expect to be able to slip away by coach with the Coalition's money?

On the other hand, if the cloud cracker *wasn't* fixing to leave by train tomorrow evening, why had Collard marked the timetable?

Quincannon took his supper at a side-street establishment called the Elite Café, which advertised "the best meal in Delford" (if this was true, the worst was probably lethal), and then walked down to the rail yards. At a quarter of seven, some of the day's heat had eased, but the sky was still summer-hazed and cloudless. A small crowd had begun to gather under the locust trees near the watchman's shack. The mood was not festive; facial expressions ranged from wary optimism to half-weary, half-sullen pessimism. It would not be long—three more days at the outside—before the more militant among the disillusioned took to cooking tar and gathering feathers.

As he approached the shack, he could hear a rumbling, fluttering noise coming from within, not unlike the activity in a hive of hornets. It had an impressive sound, as befitted a miracle cloud-cracking machine, but it was in fact nothing more than the workings of a steam boiler and galvanic battery. Noxious yellow gas still issued from the stovepipe jutting above the roof; a combination of hydrogen and oxygen produced by mingling muriatic acid, zinc, and a little hydrogen, which was then pumped skyward through the boiler. The mortar rockets contained a similar and equally worthless chemical mixture.

Quincannon was about to take up a position near the mortar platform when the shack's door opened and two men emerged. One was Ben Collard; the other, heavy set, bearded, with a flowing silver-black mane, would be the infamous Leonide Zacks. Both were in shirt sleeves, sweating profusely from the heat inside, and each carried a pair of long, slender mortar shells. Nora Zacks, dressed in a fancy green and blue outfit, a squash-blossom necklace at her throat, followed after them, smiling and waving at the crowd. Even though she, too, had been in the shack, she looked cool and dry and unruffled.

Zacks and Collard brought their burdens to the platform, laid them at the foot of the slingshot mortar. Quincannon joined them at that point; he said—"Good evening, gentlemen, Missus Zacks."—and doffed his derby to the woman. "Preparations for tonight's entertainment are nearly complete, I see."

Zacks bristled at this. He was an imposing gent up close, as most successful confidence men were; his black eyes were piercing and his manner imperious. "Entertainment?

Hardly that, sir. Hardly that. Drought breaking is serious business. And who might you be, may I ask?"

"This is Mister Quincannon, Leonide," Nora Zacks said, "the San Francisco newspaperman I told you about."

"Ah, yes." Zacks's irritation vanished behind a mask of good fellowship. He pumped Quincannon's hand vigorously. "A pleasure, sir. I am in your debt for saving my wife and assistant from harm this afternoon."

"Not at all. Mister Goodland was too far under the influence to have inflicted much harm on anyone."

"A ticklish situation, nevertheless," Zacks said. Then he frowned and said to Collard: "Here, Ben, what're you doing?"

The smaller man had climbed onto the platform, was picking up one of the rockets. Before he answered, he began inserting the missile into the cannon's muzzle. "Loading the mortar, as you can plainly see."

"There's time enough for that."

"I'd rather have done with it now."

Zacks said to Quincannon, sounding irritated again: "Insolent fellow. I may have to hire a new assistant. Now if you'll excuse me, sir, there is more work to be done inside. We'll talk again, I'm sure."

"Oh, yes. We'll have much more to say to each other later on."

Zacks turned away. Collard, who had finished loading the mortar, leaned over to take Nora Zacks's hand and help her onto the platform. Then he dropped down beside Quincannon, nodded curtly, and followed the larger man into the shack. The door shut firmly behind him.

Quincannon retraced his steps past the platform, where Nora Zacks was now soaking the tip of a long firebrand in kerosene. Under a locust tree, while he fed shag-cut tobacco into his pipe, he saw Aram Kasabian and Tom McCool approaching. O.H. Goodland was not with them, nor anywhere else among the gathered.

"We saw you talking to Zacks and Collard," the banker said when he and McCool reached him, "and wondered why."

"A testing of the waters, you might say."

"I'm not sure I. . . ."

"There isn't a speck of worry in Zacks, though I detect some in Collard. He is the dominant partner and he doesn't seem ready to skip yet."

"That's good." Kasabian looked more closely at Quincannon's face and added: "Isn't it?"

"Perhaps."

"You're still concerned about O.H.?"

"Should I be?"

"Well, he was in his room a few minutes ago. I stopped by to have a word with him."

"Sober?"

"Yes, but he was pacing like a cat. It won't surprise me if he takes it in his head to come out here tonight. . . ."

McCool said thinly: "Already has. Look."

Quincannon and the banker both turned. O.H. Goodland was striding purposefully toward the shack from the opposite direction.

At a distance he appeared grim-faced and hard-eyed. His hands were empty, but he wore his cowhide coat buttoned at the waist; it was impossible to tell if he was armed or not.

Quincannon said—"Hell and damn!"—and called out Goodland's name. The wheat farmer took no notice. He was at the shack's door now, and he beat on it once with a closed fist. It opened immediately. And immediately he pushed his way inside.

"Oh, Lord," Kasabian moaned, "if he's come to do harm to Zacks. . . ."

"Good citizens of Delford! Cover your ears and cast your eyes to the heavens! Your parched land will soon be drenched in a life-giving downpour . . . the time is at hand!"

These words came from Nora Zacks atop the platform. They brought all eyes her way, momentarily froze Quincannon and the other two men in place. She had put a lucifer to the firebrand, he saw, and now stood with it poised over the mortar's fuse vent.

McCool said in a tone of awe: "By Godfrey, the woman's fixin' to fire that thing all by herself. . . ."

He broke off as Nora Zacks lit the fuse, then dropped the firebrand, raised her skirts, and scurried down off the platform in unlady-like haste.

In the next instant there was a thunderous concussive *whump!* The slingshot cannon bucked, the platform shuddered, and the chemical rocket Collard had inserted hurtled skyward with an ear-splitting whistle. After several hundred feet the missile arced, then burst with a flash that unleashed streams of colored smoke.

Quincannon saw this at the edge of his vision; he was moving by then, his attention on the shack's closed door. It remained closed until he had gained the far end of the platform and then it popped open to reveal Ben Collard. Collard stepped out, yanked the door shut behind him; when he spied Quincannon, he began gesticulating wildly. His handsome face was a sweat-sheened mask of distress.

"Mister Quincannon!" he shouted. "Marshal McCool! Come quickly!" On the last word he spun on his heel, lunged back to the door. By the time Quincannon rushed up behind him, he had the knob in both hands and was rattling it frantically. "Locked . . . Goodland's locked it!"

"What the devil's happened?"

"He made threats, drew his pistol, and ordered me to leave. . . ." Collard pushed the door again. "Leonide! Are you all right?"

From inside a voice cried in muffled terror: "No, Goodland, no, don't shoot! Don't kill me!"

Quincannon tried to force Collard out of the way, so he could get his own hands on the knob, but the small man couldn't be budged.

McCool and Kasabian were there now, too, pushing in behind Quincannon with several other men at their heels.

Another cry came from within. "Please, spare my life!"

Seconds later there was the report of a gun.

Quincannon's reaction was immediate. He hurled his weight against Collard, with sufficient force to send the door crashing inward. Both men were off balance as they burst inside; Quincannon staggered, righted himself just in time to avoid tripping over O.H. Goodland, who was huddled on one knee on the rough plank floor. Between Goodland and the rainmaking apparatus at the far wall, Leonide Zacks lay supine in a twisted, motionless sprawl. The front of his shirt was splotched with blood.

Goodland appeared to be hurt; his face was twisted with pain and his left hand cradled the back of his head. In his right hand, held limply, was a Colt New Pocket Revolver. Quincannon yanked the weapon free of his grasp, without resistance from the farmer.

Kneeling beside Zacks, Collard said heavily: "He's dead. Shot through the heart."

The door under the boiler stood open to reveal the pulsing flames within. With all the windows closed and sealed, the heat in the room was stifling. Quincannon breathed shallowly through his mouth as he scanned the dim confines. The only light came from the fire and from a single coal-oil lamp, but his sharp eyes picked out the glint of something on the floor near one of the earthenware crocks. He side-stepped Goodland and the dead man, bent to scoop up the small object—and almost dropped it because it was hot to the touch.

A wailing voice rose from outside. "Let me through, oh, please let me through!" The knot of men clogging the doorway parted to permit the entrance of Nora Zacks. When she saw her husband, she flung herself down beside him, caught up one of his hands, and hugged it to her bosom, sobbing.

Quincannon glanced at the object he'd found. It was a spent cartridge shell. He drew out his handkerchief, wrapped the casing in it.

O.H. Goodland still clutched his scalp, grimacing, blinking now as if his eyes refused to focus properly. Dizziness overcame him when he tried to stand; he sank down again to one knee. "My head . . . feels cracked like an eggshell. . . ."

Collard said: "He must have fallen somehow when he shot poor Leonide."

"Shot? I didn't shoot anyone. . . ."

McCool stepped forward, relieved Quincannon of the Colt revolver, and peered at it. "This here's your gun, Mister Goodland."

"He's guilty as sin," Collard said. "There was no one else here, no one else could have done it. You see that, don't you, Marshal?"

"I see it," McCool agreed grimly. "Mister Goodland, I got no choice but to arrest you for the crime of murder."

Quincannon did not accompany the marshal and his

prisoner to the jailhouse. Nor did he follow Collard and a still-sobbing Nora Zacks to the hotel. Instead, he remained at the shack, waiting outside until everyone else had gone, then shutting himself inside.

The first thing he did was to examine the door and its sliding bolt. Then he searched among the jars of chemicals, spare rockets, and other items that littered the floor around the boiler and crocks; searched every nook and cranny until he satisfied himself that there was nothing else to be found, least of all the Coalition's $3,000. The money hadn't been on Zacks's person, either; he had given the body a quick frisk before the town's undertaker arrived to claim it.

From the rail yards he went to the Western Union office, where he sent a night wire to the Pinkerton agency in Chicago. The wire asked specific questions and ended with the words URGENT REPLY NEEDED. If the Pinks heeded this, as he was certain they would, he would have an answering wire early in the morning.

Warm, dusty darkness was settling when he left the telegraph office. Word of the shooting had spread quickly; gaslit Main Street was packed with citizens discussing the cloud cracker's violent demise. They would have a great deal to discuss within the next twenty-four hours, Quincannon thought as he made his way to the jailhouse to question O.H. Goodland. And they weren't the only ones with surprises in store for them.

By sundown tomorrow the name most often spoken in Delford would not be Leonide Zacks or O.H. Goodland. It would be John Quincannon.

The reply to his Chicago wire was waiting when he stopped at the telegraph office at ten o'clock Thursday morning, on his way back from a brief visit with the railroad station agent. The answers to his questions were all just as he had expected. They brought a smile to his mouth and led him to send another wire, this one to Sabina in San Francisco.

CLOUD CRACKER MURDERED LAST NIGHT IN BIZARRE CIRCUMSTANCES STOP YOUR TRUSTED PARTNER HAS ALREADY SOLVED CRIME STOP BEADLE ARRIVAL UNIMPORTANT NOW EXPECT TO REACH SF TOMORROW AS PLANNED STOP GLORIOUS WEEKEND CELEBRATION INDICATED WILL PROVIDE DETAILS OF BRILLIANT DETECTIVE WORK EN ROUTE MUIR WOODS

Whistling, his step jaunty, he crossed the street to the bank to collect Aram Kasabian. The two men then went to the jailhouse to collect Tom McCool. And the three men then proceeded to the Valley House to collect Ben Collard and Nora Zacks.

The time for unveiling his brilliant deductions had arrived.

The place for the unveiling was the marshal's tiny office, where the three of them crowded together with an unfettered and head-bandaged O.H. Goodland. Mrs. Zacks wore mourning black and a stoic expression, which remained unchanged even after Quincannon revealed his true profession, his purpose in Delford, and the upcoming arrival of Sheriff Beadle and the arrest warrants. Collard, too, seemed determined to play the innocent. He said indignantly: "This is all an intolerable misunderstanding. We are legitimate pluviculturists . . . obviously the victims of mistaken identity. We've committed no crime in the Midwest or in Delford."

"None here except willful homicide," Quincannon said.

"*Faugh!* You can't mean the murder of poor Leonide. The man who shot him has already been arrested . . . and why isn't Goodland locked in a cell where he belongs?"

"Mister Goodland did no shooting last night."

"How can you make such a statement? You were at the shack, you know what happened as well as I do. He and Leonide were locked together inside. No one else could have done it."

"But someone else did. You, Collard."

Collard drew himself up in feigned outrage. "Have you taken leave of your senses, Quincannon? I was outside with you when the shot was fired. How could I possibly be guilty?"

"By means of clever planning, careful timing, and the help of your accomplice. Or, rather, your paramour."

Nora Zacks said flatly: "That's a ridiculous accusation."

"Not at all. Your husband was a womanizer. Before the three of you left Omaha for California, his illicit affairs drove you to take his partner as your lover. His advances to Mister Goodland's daughter, successful or not, were the final straw . . . they drove you to conspire in his murder."

"Preposterous!" Collard shouted. "Nefarious!"

"Fact," Quincannon said. "As for your motives, you'd grown to hate Zacks for a different reason. He'd taken over the handling of your swindles, reduced you to a subservient role by the force of his will. With him dead, you could have his wife and his money, and be your own master again."

"Utter rot, I say."

"Mister Goodland's rash behavior two days ago gave you the impetus and the perfect foil for your plan. And the plan itself worked smoothly enough. If I hadn't come to Delford, you might well have gotten away with it . . . and with the

Coalition's three thousand dollars. Before anyone thought to ask you for the money, you and Missus Zacks would have been gone on the six o'clock train for Stockton tonight. The station agent confirmed that you purchased the tickets this morning."

"What of it? I am escorting Missus Zacks to Stockton, yes . . . but I intended to return the money before departing. Leonide's murderer is in custody, or so we thought. There is no good reason for us to stay here. . . ."

"You may have purchased the tickets today," Quincannon interrupted him, "but the date and time were settled much earlier."

"How could you possibly know that?"

"The railroad timetable in your room, the written notations in your hand. I saw them yesterday afternoon, in the course of my investigation, two hours *before* the murder."

The woman said: "That proves nothing and you know it."

"By itself, no. Tell me, Missus Zacks, why did you fire the mortar last night?"

The question took her off guard. "Why . . . I was the only person on the platform. My husband and Ben were inside the shack with Goodland."

"Why didn't you wait for them to come out?"

"The launching was scheduled for seven. Rather than delay, I went ahead on my own."

"But you'd never fired the mortar before."

"Not in Delford, but elsewhere. . . ."

"No. Your frightened actions after lighting the fuse prove otherwise. Last night was the first time and it was done by prearranged plan. That's the reason Collard loaded the mortar while I was talking to your husband . . . so it would be ready for you. Properly loading such a launcher is more difficult and dangerous than firing it."

Quincannon shifted his attention to O.H. Goodland. "Mister Goodland, why did you go to the shack after I warned you to stay away?"

"A message was slipped under the door of my room. Signed with Zacks's name and asking me to come promptly at seven to settle our differences. The word promptly was underlined."

"My husband did write such a note," Nora Zacks said. "He told me he had, which is the reason I was unconcerned when I saw Goodland arrive."

"No, Missus Zacks. The note was written by you, I suspect . . . a careful forgery."

She started to deny it, changed her mind, and said nothing.

Quincannon produced the Colt New Pocket Revolver, which McCool had let him have earlier. He showed it to Goodland and asked him: "Is this your weapon?"

"It is."

"Did you take it with you last night?"

"I did not. I had no weapon when I went to the shack, and Zacks had no damned idea what I was doing there. He was telling me that when Collard clubbed me from behind."

"When did you last have the gun in your possession?"

"Tuesday afternoon, after I made the mistake of threatening Zacks with it. McCool took it away from me."

The marshal said: "I emptied it and put it in his saddlebag at the hotel livery. Collard was there . . . he saw me do it. He could've come back later and swiped it."

"I won't stand for any more of this." Collard's voice had risen. He was sweating now. "How dare you accuse me when you know damned well it's impossible for me to be guilty. I was outside when Leonide was killed. You saw me,

Marshal. And you, Quincannon, you heard him beg for his life and you heard the fatal shot. You can't deny the truth of that."

"I can't and won't deny what I seemed to hear."

Quincannon displayed another object from his pocket. "I found this on the floor, shortly after we broke into the shack. When I picked it up, it was hot to the touch."

"Couldn't have come from Mister Goodland's gun," McCool said. "Revolvers don't eject spent shells. Only one bullet was fired from that Colt, and the empty was in the cylinder."

Kasabian asked: "Then where did that one come from?"

"The fire inside the boiler," Quincannon said, "where Collard placed it after he clubbed Mister Goodland, shot Zacks, and put the revolver in Mister Goodland's hand. A blank cartridge. The heat exploded the powder, simulating a gunshot, and the explosion kicked the casing out through the open door. Collard had used the trick before . . . I'll explain where and how shortly . . . and so he was able to gauge within a minute or so when it would go off."

"Amazing. And the shot that actually killed Zacks?"

"Fired when Missus Zacks launched the rocket promptly at seven. The boom of the mortar drowned the report. Timing, you see?"

"What about the locked door?"

"It wasn't locked. Collard pretended it was by holding onto the knob and rattling it, while he blocked the doorway with his body. The bolt wasn't damaged, a fact that was overlooked in the excitement . . . by everyone except me."

Collard knew he was caught, but in desperation he played out his last card. "Leonide was still alive when we were all inside. You know he was, you heard him beg for his life . . . you heard him!"

"No," Quincannon said, "I didn't." He paused dramatically and then asked the banker: "Mister Kasabian, do you recall my telling you Zacks and Collard were once variety performers in Chicago?"

"Yes. Low comedy and specialty acts, you said."

"I didn't know for certain what the specialty acts were until this morning, when I received a wire from the Chicago Pinkerton office. One act was a magic show in which a supposedly invisible pistol was fired on command. Zacks was the magician, Collard the one who invented and staged the trick. Collard was also a performer with his own specialty. One he performed well, by all accounts."

"What specialty, for heaven's sake?"

Quincannon said: "Ventriloquism."

Sheriff Beadle and his deputies arrived without further delay, anticlimactically, on the noon train from Fresno. By this time, even though Collard was still maintaining his innocence, Nora Zacks had admitted her part in her husband's murder. She claimed the entire plan had been Collard's and that he had coerced her into it—a falsehood, to be sure, but one she had already begun to play well with tears and lamentations. She was a comely woman; Quincannon had little doubt that she would be able to convince a jury to be lenient.

That evening he left Delford on the same train the two conspirators had intended to take, the six o'clock Limited for Stockton. He was in a fine humor. In his wallet was the balance of his fee, plus a bonus from a somewhat chastened O.H. Goodland, and in his coat pocket was a telegram from Sabina, which he had picked up at the Western Union office shortly before Beadle's arrival.

As the train rattled its way north through sun-browned

wheat fields, he took out the wire and read it again.

EAGERLY AWAIT YOUR RETURN AND DETAILS OF
BRILLIANT DETECTIVE WORK STOP HEART
AFLUTTER WITH ANTICIPATION OF GLORIOUS
WEEKEND CELEBRATION STOP DID MY HERO
COLLECT BALANCE OF FEE QM

A roguish smile split his freebooter's beard. Sabina's sarcasm didn't fool him, not for a minute. Her defenses were definitely crumbling.

Medium Rare

The night was dark, cold; most of San Francisco lay swaddled in a cloak of fog and low-hanging clouds that turned street lights and house lights into ghostly smears. The bay, close by this residential district along lower Van Ness Avenue, was invisible and the foghorns that moaned on it had a lonely, lost-soul sound. Bitter-sharp, the wind nipped at Quincannon's cheeks, fluttered his thick piratical beard as he stepped down from the hansom. A sudden gust almost tore off his derby before he could clamp it down.

A fine night for spirits, he thought wryly. The liquid kind, to be sure—except that he had been a temperance man for several years now. And the supernatural kind, in which he believed not one whit.

He helped Sabina alight from the coach, turned to survey the house at which they were about to call. It was a modest gingerbread affair, its slender front yard enclosed by a black iron picket fence. Rented, not purchased, as he had discovered earlier in the day. Gaslight flickered behind its lace-curtained front windows.

No surprise there. Professor Vargas would have been careful to select a house that had not been wired for electricity; the sometimes spectral trembles produced by gas flame were much more suited to his purposes.

On the gate was a discreet bronze sign whose raised letters gleamed faintly in the light spill from a nearby street lamp. Sabina went to peer at the sign as Quincannon paid and dismissed the hack driver. When he joined her, he, too, bent for a look.

UNIFIED COLLEGE
OF THE ATTUNED IMPULSES
Prof. A. Vargas
Spirit Medium and Counselor

"Bah. Hogwash," Quincannon said grumpily, straightening. "How can any sane person believe in such hokum?"

"Self-deception is the most powerful kind."

He made a derisive noise in his throat, a sound Sabina had once likened to the rumbling snarl of a mastiff.

She said: "If you enter growling and wearing that ferocious glare, you'll give the game away. We're here as potential devotees not ardent skeptics."

"Devotees of claptrap."

"John, Mister Buckley is paying us handsomely for this evening's work. Very handsomely, if you recall."

Quincannon recalled; his scowl faded and was replaced by a smile only those who knew him well would recognize as greed-based. Money, especially in large sums, was what soothed his savage breast. In fact, it was second only in his admiration to Sabina herself.

He glanced sideways at her. She looked even more fetching than usual this evening, dressed as she was in an outfit of black silk brocade, her raven hair topped by a stylish hat trimmed in white China silk. His mouth watered. A fine figure of a woman, Sabina Carpenter.

"John."

"*Mmm?*"

"Will you please stop staring at me that way."

"What way, my dear?"

"Like a cat at a bowl of cream. We've no time for dallying, we're late as it is. Mister Buckley and the others will be waiting to begin the séance."

Quincannon took her arm, chastely, and led her through the gate. As they mounted the front stairs, he had a clear vision of Cyrus Buckley's bank check and a clear auditory recollection of the financier's promise of the check's twin should they successfully debunk Professor Vargas and his Unified College of the Attuned Impulses.

Buckley was a reluctant follower of spiritualism, in deference to his wife who believed wholeheartedly in communication with the disembodied essences of the dead and such mediumistic double talk as "spiritual vibrations of the positive and negative forces of material and astral planes." She continually sought audiences with their daughter Bernice, the childhood victim of diphtheria, a quest that had led them to a succession of mediums and now to the most financially threatening of these paranormal spirit summoners. A recent arrival in San Francisco—from Chicago, he claimed—Vargas evidently had a more clever, extensive, and convincing repertoire of "spirit wonders" than any other medium Buckley had encountered, and of course his fees were exorbitant as a result.

The Buckleys had attended one of Vargas's sittings a few days ago—a dark séance in a locked room in his rented house. The professor had ordered himself securely tied to his chair and then proceeded to invoke a dazzling array of bell-ringing, table-tipping, spirit lights, automatic writings, ectoplasmic manifestations, and other phenomena. As his finale he announced that he was being unfettered by his friendly spirit guide and guardian, Angkar, and the rope that had bound him was heard to fly through the air just before the lights were turned up; the rope, when examined, was completely free of the more than ten knots which had been tied into it. This supernatural flim-flam had so impressed Margaret Buckley that she had returned the next day without her husband's knowledge and arranged for another sitting—tonight—and a series of private audiences at which Vargas promised to establish and maintain contact with the shade of the long-gone Bernice. Mrs. Buckley, in turn and in gratitude, was prepared to place unlimited funds in the medium's eager hands. "Endow the whole damned Unified College of the Attuned Impulses," was the way Buckley put it. Nothing he'd said or done could change his wife's mind. The only thing that would, he was convinced, was a public unmasking of the professor as the knave and charlatan he surely was. Hence, his visit to the Market Street offices of Carpenter and Quincannon, Professional Detective Services.

Quincannon had no doubt he and Sabina could accomplish the task. They had both had dealings with phony psychics before, Sabina when she was with the Pinkertons in Denver, and together on two occasions since they had opened their joint agency here. But Cyrus Buckley wasn't half so sanguine. "You'll not have an easy time of it," he'd warned them. "Professor Vargas is a rare bird and rare birds are not easily plucked. A medium among mediums."

Medium rare, is he? Quincannon thought as he twisted the doorbell handle. *Not for long. He'll not only be plucked but done to a turn before this night is over.*

The door was opened by a tiny woman of indeterminate age, dressed in a flowing ebon robe. Her skin was very white, her lips a bloody crimson in contrast; sleek brown hair was pulled tightly around her head and fastened with a jeweled barrette. Around her neck hung a silver amulet embossed with some sort of cabalistic design. "I am

Annabelle," she said in sepulchral tones. "You are Mister and Missus John Quinn?"

"We are," Quincannon said, wishing wistfully that it were true. Mr. and Mrs. John Quincannon, not Quinn. But Sabina had refused even to adopt his name for the evening's play-acting, insisting on the shortened version instead.

Annabelle took his greatcoat and Sabina's cape, hung them on a coat tree. According to Buckley, she was Professor Varga's "psychic assistant". If she lived here with him, Quincannon mused, she was likely also his wife or mistress. Seeking communion with the afterworld did not preclude indulging in the pleasures of the earthly sphere, evidently; he had never met a medium who professed to be celibate and meant it.

"Follow me, please."

They trailed her down a murky hallway into a somewhat more brightly lighted parlor. Here they found two men dressed as Quincannon was, in broadcloth and fresh linen, and two women in long fashionable dresses; one of the men was Cyrus Buckley. But it was the room's fifth occupant who commanded immediate attention.

Even Quincannon, who was seldom impressed by physical stature, had to grudgingly admit that Professor A. Vargas was a rather imposing gent. Tall, dark-complected, with a curling black mustache and piercing, almost hypnotic eyes. Like his psychic assistant, he wore a long flowing black robe and a silver amulet. On the middle fingers of each hand were two enormous glittering rings of intricate design, both of which bore hieroglyphics similar to those which adorned the amulets.

He greeted his new guests effusively, pressing his lips to the back of Sabina's hand, and then pumping Quincannon's in an iron grip. "I am Professor Vargas. Welcome, New

Ones, welcome to the Unified College of the Attuned Impulses." His voice was rich, stentorian. "Mister and Missus Quinn, is it not? Friends of the good Mister Buckley! Your first sitting but I pray not your last. You are surrounded by many anxious friends in spirit-life who desire to communicate with you once you have learned more of the laws which govern their actions. Allow your impulses to attune with theirs and your spirit friends will soon identify themselves and speak with you as in earth-life. . . ."

There was more, but Quincannon shut his ears to it.

More introductions followed the medium's windy come-on. Quincannon shook hands with red-faced, mutton-chopped Cyrus Buckley and his portly, gray-haired wife, Margaret; with Oliver Cobb, a prominent Oakland physician who bore a rather startling resemblance to the "literary hangman", Ambrose Bierce; and with Grace Cobb, the doctor's much younger and decorous wife. Decorous, that is, if a man preferred an overly buxom and overly rouged blonde to a svelte brunette of Sabina's cunning dimensions. The Cobbs, like the Buckleys, had attended the professor's previous séance.

Margaret Buckley looked upon Vargas with the rapt gaze of a supplicant in the presence of a saint. Dr. Cobb was also a true believer, judging from the look of eager anticipation he wore. The blonde Mrs. Cobb seemed to find the medium fascinating as well, but the glint in her eye was much more predatory than devout. Buckley appeared ill at ease, as if he wished the evening's business was already finished; he kept casting glances at Quincannon which the detective studiously ignored.

Vargas asked Quincannon and Sabina if they would care for a refreshment—coffee, tea, perhaps a glass of sherry. They both declined. This seemed to relieve Buckley; he asked Vargas: "Isn't it about time to begin the séance?"

"Soon, Mister Buckley. The spirits must not be hurried."

"Are they friendly tonight?" Mrs. Buckley asked. "Can you tell, dear Professor Vargas?"

"The auras are uncertain. I perceive antagonistic waves among the benign."

"Oh, Professor!"

"Do not fear," Vargas said. "Even if a malevolent spirit should cross the border, no harm will come to you or to any of us. Angkar will protect us."

"But will my Bernice's spirit be allowed through if there is a malevolent force present?"

Vargas patted her arm reassuringly. "It is my belief that she will, though I cannot be certain until the veil has been lifted. Have faith, dear Missus Buckley."

Sabina asked him: "Isn't there anything you can do to prevent a malevolent spirit from crossing over?"

"Alas, no. I am merely a teacher of the light and truth of theocratic unity, merely an operator between the beyond and this mortal sphere."

Merely a purveyor of pap, Quincannon thought.

Grace Cobb touched Vargas's sleeve; her fingers lingered almost caressingly. "We have faith in you, Professor."

"In Angkar, dear lady," Vargas told her, but his fingers caressed hers in return and the look he bestowed upon her had a smoldering quality—the same sort of cat-at-cream look, Quincannon thought, that Sabina had accused him earlier of directing at her. "Place your faith in Angkar and the spirit world."

Quincannon asked him: "Angkar is your spirit guide and guardian angel?"

"Yes. He lived more than a thousand years past and his

spirit has ascended to one of the highest planes in the after-world."

"A Hindu, was he?"

Vargas seemed mildly offended. "Not at all, my dear sir. Angkar was an Egyptian nobleman in the court of Nebuchadnezzar."

Quincannon managed to refrain from pointing out that Nebuchadnezzar was not an Egyptian but the king of Babylon and conqueror of Jerusalem some six centuries B.C. Not that any real harm would have been done if he had mentioned the fact; Vargas would have covered by claiming he had meant Nefertitti or some such. None of the others, except Sabina, perhaps, seemed to notice the error.

Sabina said: "Those rings are most impressive, Professor. Are they Egyptian?"

"This one is." Vargas presented his left hand. "An Egyptian signet and seal talisman ring, made from virgin gold. It preserves its wearer against ill luck and wicked influences." He offered his right hand. "This is the ring of King Solomon. Its Chaldaic inscription stands as a reminder to the wearer that no matter what his troubles may be, they shall soon be gone. The inscription . . . here . . . translates as 'This shall also pass'."

"Oh, Professor Vargas," Mrs. Buckley gushed, "you're so knowledgeable, so wise in so many ways."

Quincannon's dinner stirred uneasily under his breastbone.

He was spared further discomfort, at least for the present, by the entrance of the psychic assistant, Annabelle. She announced—"All is in readiness, Professor."—and, without waiting for a response, glided out again.

"Good ladies and gentlemen," Vargas said, "before we enter the spirit room may I accept your most kind and welcome donations to the Unified College of the Attuned Impulses, so that we may continue in our humble efforts to bring the psychic and material planes into closer harmony?"

Quincannon paid for himself and Sabina—the outrageous "New Ones" donation of $50 each. If he had not been assured of reimbursement from their client, he would have been much more grudging than he was in handing over the greenbacks. Buckley was tight-lipped as he paid, and sweat oiled his neck and the lower of his two chins; the look he gave Quincannon was a mute plea not to botch the job he and Sabina had been hired to do. Only Dr. Cobb ponied up with what appeared to be genuine satisfaction.

The medium casually dropped the wad of bills onto a table, as if money mattered not in the slightest to him personally, and led them out of the parlor, down the gloomy hallway, and then into a large chamber at the rear. The spirit room contained quite a few more accoutrements than the parlor, of greater variety and a more unusual nature. The floor was covered by a thick Oriental carpet of dark blue and black design. Curtains made of the same ebon material as the professor's and Annabelle's robes blotted the windows, and the gaslight had been turned low enough so that shadows crouched in all four corners. The overheated air was permeated with the smell of incense; Quincannon, who hated the stuff, immediately began to breathe through his mouth. The incense came from a burner on the mantel of a small fireplace—a horsey-looking bronze monstrosity with tusks as well as equine teeth and a shaggy mane and beard.

The room's centerpiece was an oval, highly polished table around which six straight-backed chairs were arranged; a seventh chair, larger than the others, with a high seat and arms raised on a level with that of the table top, was placed at the head. Along the walls were a short, narrow sideboard of Oriental design, made of teak, with an intricately inlayed center top; a tall-backed rococo love seat; and an alabaster pedestal atop which sat a hideous bronze statue of an Egyptian male in full headdress—a representation, evidently, of the mythical Angkar. In the middle of the table was a clear-glass jar, a tiny silver bell suspended inside. On the sideboard were a silver tray containing several bottles of various sizes and shapes, a tambourine, and a stack of children's school slates in black wooden frames. Propped against the wall nearby was an ordinary-looking three-stringed guitar. And on the high seat of the armchair lay a coil of sturdy rope Quincannon estimated as some three yards in length.

When the sitters were all inside and loosely grouped near the table, Vargas closed the door, produced a large brass key from a pocket in his robe, and proceeded with a flourish to turn the key in the latch. After which he brought the key to the sideboard and set it beside the tray in plain sight. While this was being done, Quincannon eased over in front of the door and tested it behind his back to determine if it was in fact locked. It was.

Still at the sideboard, Vargas announced that before they formed the "mystic circle" two final preparations were necessary. Would one of the good believers be so kind as to assist him in the first of these? Quincannon stepped forward just ahead of Dr. Cobb.

The medium said: "Mister Quinn, will you kindly examine each of the slates you see before you and tell us if they are as they seem . . . ordinary writing slates?"

Quincannon examined them more carefully than any of the devotees would have. "Quite ordinary," he said.

"Select two, if you please, write your name on each with

this slate pencil, and then place them together and tie them securely with your handkerchief."

When Quincannon had complied, Vargas took the bound slates and placed them in the middle of the stack. "If the spirits are willing," he said, "a message will be left for you beneath the signatures. Perhaps a loved one who has passed beyond the pale, perhaps from a friendly sprite who may be in tune with your particular psychic impulses. Discarnate forces are never predictable, you understand."

Quincannon nodded and smiled with his teeth.

"We may now be seated and form the mystic circle."

When each of the sitters had selected and was standing behind a chair, Sabina to the medium's immediate left and Quincannon directly across from him, both by prearrangement, Vargas again called for a volunteer. This time it was Dr. Cobb who stepped up first. Vargas handed him the coiled rope and seated himself in the high chair, his forearms flat on the chair arms with only his wrists and hands extended beyond the edges. He then instructed Cobb to bind him securely—arms, legs, and chest—to the chair, using as many knots as possible. Quincannon watched closely as this was done. He caught Sabina's eye when the doctor was finished; she dipped her chin to acknowledge that she, too, had spotted the gaffe in this phase of the professor's game.

Cobb, with Buckley's help, moved Vargas's chair closer to the table, so that his hands and wrists rested on the surface. Smiling, the medium asked the others to take their seats. As Quincannon sat down, he bumped against the table, then reached down to feel of one of its legs. As he'd expected, the table was much less heavy than it appeared to be at a glance. He stretched out a leg and with the toe of his shoe explored the carpet. The floor beneath seemed to be solid, but the nap was thick enough so that he couldn't be certain.

Vargas instructed everyone to spread their hands, the fingers of the left to grasp the wrist of the person on that side; thus one hand of each person was holding and the other was being held. "Once we begin," he said, "attempt to empty your minds of all thought, to keep them as blank as the table's surface throughout. And remember, you must not move either hands or feet during the séance . . . you must not under any circumstances break the mystic circle. To do so could have grave consequences. There have been instances where inattention and disobedience have been fatal to sensitives such as myself."

The professor closed his eyes, let his chin lower slowly to his chest. After a few seconds he commenced a whispering chant, a mixture of English and simulated Egyptian in which he called for the door to the spirit world to open and the shades of the departed to pass through and reveal their presence. While this was going on, the lights began to dim as if in phantasmical response to Vargas's exhortations. The phenomenon elicited a shivery gasp from Margaret Buckley, but Quincannon was unimpressed. Gaslight in the room was easily controlled from another—in this case by the assistant, Annabelle, at a prearranged time or on some sort of signal.

The shadows congealed until the room was in utter darkness. Vargas's chanting ceased abruptly; the silence deepened as it lengthened. Long minutes passed with no sounds except for the somewhat asthmatic breathing of Cyrus Buckley, the rustle of a dress or shuffle of a foot on the carpet. A palpable tension began to build. Sweat formed on Quincannon's face, not from any tension but from the overheated air. He was not a man given to fancies, but he was forced to admit that there was an eerie quality to sitting in total blackness this way, waiting for something to happen. Spiritualist mediums counted on this reaction, of course. The more keyed up their dupes became, the more eager they were to believe in the incredible things they were about to witness, and the more eager they were, the more easily they could be fooled by their own senses.

Someone coughed, a sudden sharp sound that made even Quincannon twitch involuntarily. He thought the cough had come from Vargas, but in such stifling darkness you couldn't be certain of the direction of any sound. Even when the medium spoke again, the words might have come from anywhere in the room.

"Angkar is with us. I feel his presence."

On Quincannon's left, Dr. Cobb stirred and their knees bumped together; Mrs. Buckley, on his right, brought forth another of her shivery gasps.

"Will you speak to us tonight, Angkar? Will you answer our questions in the language of the dead and guide us among your fellow spirits? Please grant our humble request. Please answer yes."

The silver bell inside the jar rang once, muted but clear.

"Angkar has consented. He will speak, he will lead us. He will ring the bell once for yes to each question he is asked, twice for no, for that is the language of the dead. Will someone ask him a question? Doctor Cobb?"

"I will," Cobb's voice answered. "Angkar, is my brother Philip well and happy on the Other Side?"

The bell tinkled once.

"Will he appear to us in his spirit form?"

Yes.

"Will it be tonight?"

Silence.

Vargas said: "Angkar is unable to answer that question yet. Please ask another."

There was a good deal of this, with questions from Cobb, his wife, and Mrs. Buckley. Then Vargas called on Sabina to ask the spirit guide a question.

She obliged by saying: "Angkar, tell me please, is my little boy John with you? He was always such a bad little boy that I fear for his poor troubled soul."

Yes, he is one of us.

No, he is not here tonight.

"Has he learned humility and common sense, two qualities which he lacked on this early sphere?"

Yes.

"And has he learned to take no for an answer?"

Yes.

Quincannon scowled in the darkness. Although Sabina had been married once, she had no children. The "little boy John" was her doting partner, of course. Having a bit of teasing fun at his expense while at the same time establishing proof of Vargas's deceit.

"Mister Quinn?" the professor said. "Will you ask Angkar a question?"

He might not have responded as he did if the heat and the sickly sweet incense hadn't given him a headache. But his head throbbed, and Sabina's playfulness rankled, and the words were out of his mouth before he could bite them back. "Oh, yes, indeed," he said. "Angkar, will my dear wife ever consent to share my cold and lonely bed?"

Shocked murmurs, a muffled choking sound that might have come from Sabina. The bell was silent. And then, without warning, the table seemed to stir and tremble beneath Quincannon's outstretched hands. Its smooth surface rippled; a faint creak sounded from somewhere underneath.

In the next instant the table tilted sideways, turned and rocked and wobbled as if it had been injected with a life of its own. The agitated movements continued for several seconds, stopped altogether—and then the table lifted completely off the floor, seemed to float in the air for another two or three heartbeats before finally thudding back onto the carpet.

Throughout all of this, the silver bell inside the jar remained conspicuously silent.

"Mister Quinn, you have angered Angkar." The medium's voice was sharply reproachful. "He finds your question inappropriate, frivolous, even mocking. He may deny us further communication, and return to the afterworld."

Mrs. Buckley cried: "Oh, no, please, he mustn't go!"

Cobb said angrily: "Damn your eyes, Quinn. . . ."

"Silence!" Vargas, in a sibilant whisper. "We must do nothing more to disturb the spirits or the consequences may be dire. Do not move or speak. Do not break the circle."

The stuffy blackness closed down again. It was an effort for Quincannon to hold still. He regretted his question, although not because of any effect on Angkar and his discarnate legion; he was sure that the table tipping and levitation would have taken place in any event. His regret was that he had allowed Sabina to glimpse the depth of his frustration, and unto the bargain added weight to her already erroneous idea of the nature of his passion. Seduction wasn't his game; his affection for her was genuine, abiding. Hell and damn! Now it might take him days, even weeks to undo the damage done by his profligate tongue. . . .

A sound burst the heavy stillness, a jingling that was not of the silver bell in the jar. The tambourine that had been on the sideboard. Its jingling continued, steady, almost musical in an eerily discordant way.

Vargas's whisper was fervent. "Angkar is still present. He has forgiven Mister Quinn, permitted us one more chance to communicate with the spirits he has brought with him."

Mrs. Buckley: "Praise Angkar! Praise the spirits!"

The shaking of the tambourine ended. And all at once a ghostly light appeared at a distance overhead, pale and vaporous; hovered, and then commenced a swirling motion that created faint luminous streaks on the wall of dead black. One of the sitters made an ecstatic throat noise. The swirls slowed, the light stilled again for a moment, then it began to rise until it seemed to hover just below the ceiling; at last it faded away entirely. Other lights, mere pinpricks, flicked on and off, moving this way and that as if a handful of fireflies had been released in the room.

A thin, moaning wail erupted.

The pinpricks of light vanished.

Quincannon, listening intently, heard a faint ratchety noise followed by a strumming chord. The vaporous light reappeared, now in a different location closer to the floor; at the edge of its glow the guitar could be seen to leap into the air, to gyrate this way and that with no hand upon it. The strumming chord replayed and was joined by others— strange music that sounded and yet did not sound as though it were being made by the strings.

For three, four, five seconds the guitar continued its levitating dance, seemingly playing a tune upon itself. Then the glow once more faded, and, when it was gone, the music ceased and the guitar twanged to rest on the carpet.

Nearly a minute passed in electric silence.

Grace Cobb shrieked: "A hand! I felt a hand brush against my cheek!"

Vargas warned: "Do not move, do not break the circle."

Something touched Quincannon's neck, a velvety caress

that lifted the short hairs there and bristled them like a cat's fur. If the fingers—they felt exactly like cold, lifeless fingers—had lingered, he would have ignored the professor's remonstration and made an attempt to grab and hold onto them. But the hand or whatever it was slid away almost immediately.

Moments later it materialized long enough for it to be identifiable as just that—a disembodied hand. Then it was gone as if it had never been there at all.

Another period of silence.

The unearthly moan again.

And a glowing face appeared, as disembodied as the hand, above where Dr. Cobb sat.

The face was a man's, shrouded as if in a band of whitish drapery that ran right around it and was cut off at a straight line on the lower part. The eyes were enormous black-rimmed holes. The mouth moved, formed words in a deep-throated rumble.

"Oliver? It's Philip, Oliver."

"Philip! I'm so glad you've come at long last." Cobb's words were choked with feeling. "Are you well?"

"I am well. But I cannot stay long. The Auras have allowed me to make contact but now I must return."

"Yes . . . yes, I understand."

"I will come again. For a longer visit next time, Oliver. Next time. . . ."

The face was swallowed by darkness.

More minutes crept away. Quincannon couldn't tell how many; he had lost all sense of time and space in the suffocating dark.

A second phantom-like countenance materialized, this one high above Margaret Buckley's chair. It was shimmery, indistinct behind a hazy substance like a luminous veil. The words that issued from it were in an otherworldly, child-like quaver—the voice of a little girl.

"Mommy! Is that you, Mommy?"

"Oh thank God! Bernice!" Margaret Buckley's cry was rapturous. "Cyrus, it's our darling Bernice!"

Her husband made no response.

"I love you, Mommy. Do you love me?"

"Oh yes! Bernice, dearest, I prayed and prayed you'd come. Are you happy in the afterworld? Tell Mommy."

"Yes, I'm very happy. But I must go back now."

"No, not so soon! Bernice, wait. . . ."

"Will you come again, Mommy? Promise me you'll come again. Then the Auras will let me come, too."

"I'll come, darling, I promise!"

The radiant image vanished.

Mrs. Buckley began to weep softly.

Quincannon was fed up with this hokum. Good and angry, too. It was despicable enough for fake mediums to dupe the gullible, but when they resorted to the exploitation of a middle-aged woman's yearning for her long-dead child, the game became intolerable. The sooner he and Sabina put finish to it, the better for all concerned. If there was even one more materialization. . . .

There wasn't. He heard scratchings, the unmistakable sound of the slate pencil writing on a slate. This was followed by yet another protracted silence, broken only by the faintest of scraping and clicking sounds that Quincannon couldn't identify.

Vargas said abruptly: "The spirits have grown restless. All except Angkar are returning now to the land beyond the border. Angkar will leave, too, but first he will free me from my bonds, just as one day we will all be freed from our mortal ties. . . ."

The last word was chopped off in a meaty smacking noise and an explosive grunt of pain. Another smack, a gurgling moan.

Sabina cried out in alarm: "John! Something's happened to Vargas!" Other voices rose in frightened confusion. Quincannon pushed up from the table, fumbling in his pocket for a lucifer. His thumbnail scratched it alight.

In the smoky flare he saw the others scrambling to their feet around the table, all except Professor Vargas. The medium, still roped to his chair, was slumped forward with his chin on his chest, unmoving. Quincannon kicked his own chair out of the way, carried the lucifer across to the nearest wall sconce. The gas was off; he turned it on and applied the flame. Flickery light burst forth, chasing shadows back into the room's corners.

Outside in the hallway, hands began to beat on the door panel. Annabelle's voice rose shrilly: "Let me in! I heard a cry . . . let me in!"

"Dear Lord, he's been stabbed!"

The exclamation came from Cyrus Buckley. There were other cries overridden by a shriek from Mrs. Buckley; Quincannon turned in time to see her swoon in her husband's arms. He ran to where Sabina stood staring down at the medium's slumped body.

Stabbed, for a fact. The weapon, a dagger whose ornate hilt bore a series of hieroglyphics, jutted from the back of his neck. Another wound, the first one struck for it still oozed blood, showed through a rent in Vargas's robe lower down, between the shoulder blades.

Ashen-faced, Dr. Cobb bent to feel for a pulse in the professor's neck. He shook his head and said—"Expired."—a few moments later.

"It isn't possible," his wife whispered. "How *could* he have been stabbed?"

Buckley had lowered his wife onto one of the chairs and was fanning her flushed face with his hand. He said shakily: "How . . . and by whom?"

Quincannon caught Sabina's eye. She wagged her head to tell him she didn't know, or couldn't be sure, what had happened in those last few seconds of darkness.

The psychic assistant, Annabelle, was still beating on the door, clamoring for admittance. Quincannon went to the sideboard. The brass key lay where Vargas had set it down before the séance began; he used it to unlock the door. Annabelle rushed in from the dark hallway, her eyes wide and fearful. She gave a little moan when she saw Vargas and ran to his side, knelt to peer into his dead face.

When she straightened again, her own face was as white as milk. She said tremulously: "One of you did this?"

"No," Dr. Cobb told her. "It couldn't have been one of us. No one broke the circle until after the professor was stabbed."

"Then . . . it was the spirits."

"He did perceive antagonistic waves tonight. But why would a malevolent spirit . . . ?"

"He made all the Auras angry. I warned him but he didn't listen."

Sabina said: "How did he make the Auras angry, Annabelle?"

The woman shuddered and shook her head. Then her eyes shifted into a long stare across the room. "The slates," she said.

"What about the slates?"

"Did the spirits leave a message? Have you looked?"

Quincannon swung around to the sideboard; the others, except for Margaret Buckley, crowded closely behind him. The tied slates were in the center of the stack where Vargas had placed them. He lifted those two out, undid the knot in his handkerchief, parted them for his eyes and the eyes of the others.

Murmurs and a mildly blasphemous exclamation from Buckley.

In a ghost-like hand beneath the "John Quinn" signatures on each, one message upside down and backwards as if it were a mirror image of the other, was written: **I Angkar destroyed the evil one.**

"Angkar!" Dr. Cobb said. "Why would the professor's guide and guardian turn on him that way?"

"The spirits are not mocked," Annabelle said. "They know evil when it is done in their name and then guardian becomes avenger."

"Madame, what are you saying?"

"I warned him," she said again. "He would not listen and now he has paid the price. His torment will continue on the Other Side, until his essence has been cleansed of wickedness."

Quincannon said—"Enough talk and speculation."—in authoritarian tones that swiveled all heads in his direction. "There'll be time for that later. Now there's work to be done."

"Quite right," Cobb agreed. "The police. . . ."

"Not the police, Doctor. Not yet."

"Here, Quinn, who are you to take charge?"

"The name isn't Quinn, it's Quincannon. John Quincannon. Of Carpenter and Quincannon, Professional Detective Services."

Cobb gaped at him. "A detective? You?"

"Two detectives." He gestured to Sabina. "My partner, Missus Carpenter."

"A *woman?*" Grace Cobb said. She sounded as if Sabina had been revealed as a soiled dove.

Sabina, testily: "And why not, pray tell?"

Dr. Cobb: "Who hired you? Who brought you here under false pretenses?"

Quincannon and Sabina both looked at Buckley. To his credit, the financier wasted no time in admitting he was their client.

"You, Cyrus?" Margaret Buckley had revived and was regarding them dazedly. "I don't understand. Why would you engage detectives?"

Before her husband could reply, Quincannon said: "Mister Buckley will explain in the parlor. Be so good, all of you, as to go there and wait."

"For what?" Cobb demanded.

"For Missus Carpenter and me to do what no other detective, police officer, or private citizen can do half as well." False modesty was not one of Quincannon's character flaws, despite Sabina's occasional attempts to convince him otherwise. "Solve a baffling crime."

No one protested, although Dr. Cobb wore an expression of disapproval and Annabelle said—"What good are earthly detectives when it is the spirits who have taken vengeance?"—as they left the room. Within a minute Quincannon and Sabina were alone with the dead man.

He turned the key in the lock to insure their privacy. He said then: "Well, my dear, a pretty puzzle, eh?"

Instead of answering, Sabina fetched him a stinging slap that rattled his eyelids. "That," she said, "is for the rude remark about sharing your bed."

For once, he was speechless. He might have argued that

she had precipitated the remark with her own sly comments, but this was neither the time nor the place. Besides, he could not recall ever having won an argument with Sabina over anything of consequence. There had been numerous draws, yes, but never a clear-cut victory.

"Now, then," she said briskly, "shall we see if we can make good on your boast?"

They proceeded, first to extinguish the incense burner and to open a window so that cold night air could refresh the room, and then with an examination of the walls, fireplace, and floor. All were solid; there were no secret openings, crawl spaces, hidey holes, or trap doors. Quincannon then went to inspect the corpse, while Sabina examined the jar-encased bell on the table.

The first thing he noticed was that, although the rope still bound Professor Vargas to his chair, it was somewhat loose across forearms and sternum. When he lifted the limp left hand, he found that it had been freed of the bonds. Vargas's right foot had also been freed. Confirmation of his suspicions in both cases. He had also more or less expected his next discovery, the two items concealed inside the sleeve of the medium's robe.

He was studying the items when Sabina said: "Just as I thought. The jar was fastened to the table with gum adhesive."

"Can you pry it loose?"

"I already have. The clapper on the bell. . . ."

". . . is either missing or frozen. Eh?"

"Frozen. Vargas used another bell to produce his spirit rings, obviously."

"This one." Quincannon held up the tiny hand bell with its gauze-muffled clapper. "Made and struck so as to produce a hollow ring, as if it were coming from the bell inside the jar. The directionless quality of sounds in total darkness, and the power of suggestion, completed the deception."

"What else have you got there?"

He showed her the second item from Vargas's sleeve.

"A reaching rod," she said. "*Mmm*, yes."

Quincannon said: "His left hand was holding yours on the table. Could you tell when he freed it?"

"No, and I was waiting for just that. I think he may have done it when he coughed. You recall?"

"I do."

"He was really quite cunning," Sabina said. "A charlatan among charlatans, to paraphrase Mister Buckley."

Medium rare, Quincannon thought again, *and now medium dead. Plucked and done to a turn, for a fact, though not at all in the way anticipated.* "Have you a suggestion as to who stabbed him?"

"None yet, except that it wasn't Angkar or any other supernatural agency. Annabelle may believe in spirits who wield daggers, but I don't."

"Nor I."

"One of the others at the table. A person clever enough to break the circle in the same way Vargas did and then to stand up, commit the deed, and return to his chair . . . all in utter darkness."

"Doesn't seem possible, does it."

"No more impossible than any of the other humbug we witnessed tonight. We've encountered such enigmas before, John."

"Too often for my liking. Well, we already have some of the answers to the evening's queer show. Find the rest and we'll solve the riddle of Vargas's death as well."

One of the missing answers came from an examination of

the professor's mystic rings. The one on his left hand that he had referred to as an Egyptian signet and seal talisman ring had a hidden fingernail catch; when it was flipped, the entire top hinged upward to reveal a small sturdy hook within. Quincannon had no doubt that were he to get down on all fours and peer under the table where the medium sat, he would find a tiny metal eye screwed to the wood.

The miraculous self-playing guitar, which of course was nothing of the kind, drew him next. He already knew how its dancing levitation had been managed; a close scrutiny of the instrument revealed the rest of the gaffe.

"John, look at this."

Sabina was at the sideboard, fingering a small bottle. When he'd set the guitar down and joined her, he saw that she had removed the bottle's glass stopper. "This was among the others on the tray," she told him, and held it up for him to sniff its contents.

"Ah," he said. "Almond oil."

"Mixed with white phosphorous, surely."

He nodded. "The contents of the other bottles?"

"Liquor and incense oils. Nothing more than window dressing."

Quincannon stood looking at the sideboard. At length he knelt and ran his hands over its smooth front, its fancily inlayed center top. There seemed to be neither doors nor a way to lift open the top, as if the sideboard might be a sealed wooden box. This proved not to be the case, however. It took him several minutes to locate the secret spring catch, cleverly concealed as it was among the dark-squared inlays. As soon as he pressed it, the catch released noiselessly and the entire top slid up and back on oiled hinges.

The interior was a narrow, hollow space—a box, in fact, that seemed more like a child's toy than a sideboard. A clutch of items were pushed into one corner. Quincannon lifted them out one by one.

A yard or two of white silk.

Another yard of fine white netting, so fine that it could be wadded into a ball no larger than a walnut.

A two-foot square piece of black cloth.

A small container of safety matches.

A theatrical mask.

And a pair of rubber gloves almost but not quite identical, both of which had been stuffed with cotton and dipped in melted paraffin.

He returned each item to the sideboard, finally closed the lid. He said with satisfaction: "That leaves only the writing on the slates. And we know now how that was done, don't we, my dear?"

"And how Professor Vargas was murdered."

"And by whom."

They smiled at each other. Smiles that gleamed wolfishly in the trembling gaslight.

Neither the Buckleys nor the Cobbs took kindly to being ushered back into the séance room, even though Quincannon had moved both Vargas's body and chair away from the table and draped them with a cloth Sabina had found in another room. There was some grumbling when he asked them to assume their former positions around the table, but they all complied. A seventh chair had been added to Vargas's place; he invited Annabelle to sit there. She, too, complied, maintaining a stoic silence.

Buckley asked: "Will this take long, Quincannon? My wife has borne the worst of this ordeal. She isn't well."

"Not long, Mister Buckley, I assure you."

"Is it absolutely necessary for us to be in here?"

"It is." Quincannon looked around at the others. "We have nothing to fear from the dead, past or present. The spirits were not responsible for what took place here tonight. Not any of it."

Grace Cobb: "Are you saying one of us stabbed Professor Vargas?"

"I am."

Annabelle: "No. It was Angkar. You mustn't deny the spirits. The penalties. . . ."

"A pox on the penalties," Quincannon said. "Professor Vargas was murdered by a living, flesh-and-blood individual."

Dr. Cobb: "Who? If you're so all-fired certain it was one of us, name him."

"Perhaps it was you, Doctor."

"See here . . . ! What motive could I possibly have?"

"Any one of several. Such as a discovery prior to tonight that Vargas was a fake. . . ."

"A fake!"

". . . and you were so enraged by his duplicity that you determined to put a stop to it once and for all."

"Preposterous."

Quincannon was enjoying himself now. Dramatic situations appealed to his nature; he was, as Sabina had more than once pointed out, a bit of a ham. He turned his gaze on Grace Cobb. "Or you, Missus Cobb. Perhaps you're the guilty party."

She regarded him haughtily. "If that is an accusation. . . ."

"Not at all. Merely a suggestion of possibility, of hidden motives of your own." Such as an interest in the medium that had gone beyond the spiritual and ended in a spurned lover's—or even a blackmail victim's—murderous rage.

"Or it could be you, Mister Buckley, and your hiring of Carpenter and Quincannon but a smoke screen to hide your lethal intentions for this evening."

The financier's eyes glittered with anger. Sabina said warningly: "That'll do, John."

"It had better do," Buckley said. "If you entertain any hope of receiving the balance of your fee. You know full well neither I nor my wife ended that scoundrel's life."

Dr. Cobb: "I don't see how it could have been any of us. We were all seated here . . . all except Annabelle, and she was on the other side of the locked door. And none of us broke the circle."

"Are you certain of that, Doctor?" Quincannon asked.

"Of course, I'm certain."

"But you're wrong. Vargas himself broke it."

"That's impossible."

"Not at all. Neither impossible nor difficult to manage."

"*Why* would he do such a thing? For a medium to break the mystic circle is to risk the wrath of the spirits, endanger his own life. He told us so himself."

"He had already incurred the wrath of the Auras," Annabelle said fervidly. "It was Angkar, I tell you. Angkar who plunged the dagger into his body. . . ."

Quincannon ignored her. He said to no one in particular: "You don't seem to have grasped my words to you a minute ago. Professor Vargas was a fake. The Unified College of the Attuned Impulses is a fake. He was no more sensitive to the spirit world than you or I or President Cleveland."

"That . . . that can't be true!" Margaret Buckley's face was strained, her eyes feverish. "Everything we saw and heard tonight . . . the visitations . . . my daughter. . . ."

"Sham and illusion, the lot of it," Sabina said gently.

"I'm sorry, Missus Buckley."

"But . . . but how?"

"We'll explain," Quincannon told her, "all of Vargas's tricks during the séance. To begin with, the way in which he freed his left hand while seeming to maintain an unbroken clasp of hands.

"The essence of that trick lies in the fact that the hand consists of both a wrist and fingers and the wrist is able to bend in different directions. The fingers of Vargas's left hand, you remember, were holding Missus Carpenter's wrist, while Missus Cobb's fingers were gripping his right wrist. By maneuvering his hands closer and closer together as he talked, in a series of small spasmodic movements, he also brought the ladies' hands closer together. When they were near enough for his own thumbs to touch, he freed his left hand in one quick movement and immediately reestablished control with his right . . . the same hand's fingers holding Missus Carpenter while its wrist was being gripped by Missus Cobb."

Buckley: "But how could he manage that when we were all concentrating on tight control?"

"He coughed once, rather loudly, if you recall. The sound was a calculated aural distraction. In that instant . . . and an instant was all it took . . . he completed the maneuver. He also relied on the fact that a person's senses become unreliable after a protracted period of sitting in total darkness. What you think you see, hear, feel at any given moment may in fact be partly or completely erroneous."

There was a brief silence while others digested this. Dr. Cobb said then: "Even with one hand free, how could he have rung the spirit bell? I bound him myself, Quincannon, and I am morally certain the loops and knots were tight."

"You may be certain in your own mind, Doctor, but the

facts are otherwise. It is a near impossibility for anyone, even a professional detective, to securely tie a man to a chair with a single length of rope. And you were flurried, self-conscious, anxious to acquit yourself well of the business, and you are a gentleman besides. You would hardly bind a man such as Professor Vargas, who you admired and respected, with enough constriction of the rope to cut into his flesh. A fraction of an inch of slack is all a man who had been tied many times before, who is skilled in muscular control, requires in order to free one hand."

Cobb was unable to refute the logic of this. He lapsed into a somewhat daunted silence as Quincannon went on to explain and demonstrate the bell-ringing trick.

"Next we have the table tipping and levitation. Vargas accomplished this phenomenon with but one hand and one foot, the right lower extremity having been freed with the aid of the upper left." Quincannon had removed the Egyptian talisman ring from the medium's finger; he held it up, released the fingernail catch to reveal the hook within. "He attached this hook to a small eye screwed beneath the table, after which he gave a sharp upward jerk. The table legs on his end were lifted off the carpet just far enough for him to slip the toe of his shoe under one of them, thus creating a human clamp which gave him full control of the table. By lifting with his ring and elevating his toe while the heel remained on the carpet, he was able to make the table tilt, rock, gyrate at will."

Sabina added: "And when he was ready for the table to appear to levitate, he simply unhooked his ring and thrust upward with his foot, withdrawing it immediately afterward. The illusion of the table seeming to float under our hands for a second or two before it fell was enhanced by both the circumstances and the darkness."

Buckley, with some bitterness: "Seems so blasted obvious when explained."

"Such flummery always is, Mister Buckley. It's the trappings and manipulation that make it mystifying. The so-called spirit lights are another example." Sabina placed the stoppered glass bottle on the table and described where she'd found it and what it contained. "Mix white phosphorous with any fatty oil, and the result is a bottle filled with hidden light. As long as the bottle remains stoppered, the phosphorous gives off no glow, but as soon as the cork is removed and air is permitted to reach the phosphorous, a faint unearthly shine results. Wave the bottle in the air and the light seems to dart about. Replace the stopper and the light fades away as the air inside is used up."

"The little winking lights were more of the same, I suppose?"

"Not quite," Quincannon said. "Match heads were their source. Hold a match head between the moistened forefinger and thumb of each hand, wiggle the forefinger enough to expose and then once more quickly conceal the match head, and you have flitting fireflies."

Grace Cobb asked: "The guitar that seemed to dance and play itself . . . how was that done?"

Quincannon fetched the guitar, brought it back to the table. Beside it he set the reaching rod from Vargas's sleeve. The rod was only a few inches in length when closed, but when he opened out each of its sections after the fashion of a telescope, it extended the full length of the table and beyond—more than six feet overall. "Vargas extended this rod in his left hand," he said, "inserted it in the hole in the neck of the instrument, raised and slowly turned the guitar this way and that to create the illusion of air-dancing. As for the music. . . ."

He reached into the hole under the strings, gave it a quick twist. The weird strumming they had heard during the séance began to emanate from within.

Mrs. Cobb: "A music box!"

"A one-tune music box, to be precise, affixed to the wood inside with gum adhesive."

Buckley: "The hand that touched Missus Cobb's cheek? The manifestations? The spirit writing on the slate?"

"All part and parcel of the flummery," Quincannon told him. Again he went to the sideboard, where he pressed the hidden release to raise its top. From inside he took out the two stuffed and wax-coated rubber gloves, held them up for the others to view.

"These are the ghostly fingers that touched Missus Cobb and my neck as well. The smoothness of the paraffin gives them the feel of human flesh. One hand has been treated with luminous paint . . . it was kept covered under this"— he showed them the black cloth—"until the time came to reveal it as a glowing disembodied entity."

He lifted out the silk drapery and theatrical mask. "The mask has been treated in the same way. The combination of these two items were used to create the manifestation alleged to be Philip Cobb."

He raised the fine white netting. "Likewise made phosphorescent and draped over the head to create the manifestation purported to be the Buckleys' daughter."

"But . . . I heard Bernice speak," Margaret Buckley said weakly. "It was her voice, I'm sure it was. . . ."

Her husband took her hand in both of his. "No, Margaret, it wasn't. You only imagined it to be."

"An imitation of a child's voice," Quincannon said, "just as the other voice was an imitation of a man's deep articulation."

He picked up the two slates which bore the spirit message under his false signatures. " 'I, Angkar destroyed the evil one.' Vargas's murderer wrote those words, in sequence on one slate and upside down and backwards on the other to heighten the illusion of spirit writing. *Before* the murder was done, in anticipation of it."

"Who?" Buckley demanded. "Name the person, Quincannon."

"Professor Vargas's accomplice, of course."

"Accomplice?"

"Certainly. No one individual, no matter how skilled in supernatural fakery, could have arranged and carried out all the tricks we were subjected to even if he *hadn't* been roped to his chair. Someone else had to direct the reaching rod to the guitar and then turn the spring on the music box. Someone else had to jangle the tambourine, make the wailing noises, carry the phosphorous bottle to different parts of the room and up onto the love seat there so as to make the light seem to float near the ceiling. Someone else had to manipulate the waxed gloves, don the mask and drapery and netting, imitate the spirit voices."

"Annabelle! Are you saying it was Annabelle?"

"None other."

They all stared at the pale, silent woman at the head of the table. Her expression remained frozen, but her gaze burned with a zealot's fire.

Dr. Cobb said: "But she wasn't in the room with us. . . ."

"Ah, but she was, Doctor. At first I believed her to have been in another part of the house . . . not because of the locked door but because of the way in which the lights dimmed and extinguished to begin the séance. It seemed she must have turned the gas off at a prearranged time. Not so. Some type of automatic timing mechanism was used for that purpose. Annabelle, you see, was already present here *before* the rest of us entered and Vargas locked the door."

"Before, you say?"

"She disappeared from the parlor, you'll recall, as soon as she announced that all was in readiness. While Vargas detained us with his call for donations, Annabelle slipped into this room and hid herself."

"Where? There are no hiding places . . . unless you expect us to believe she crawled up inside the fireplace chimney."

"Not there, no. Nor are there any secret closets or passages or any other such hocus-pocus. She was hidden. . . ."

". . . in the same place as her spirit props," Sabina interrupted, "within the sideboard." Her testy glance at Quincannon said he'd hogged center stage long enough; she wasn't above a bit of a flare for the dramatic herself, he thought fondly. "The interior is hollow, and she is both tiny and enough of a contortionist to fold her body into such a short, narrow space. The catch that releases the hinged top can be operated from within as well. Once the room was in total darkness and Vargas began invoking the spirits, she climbed out to commence her preparations. Under her robe, I'll warrant, is an all-black, close-fitting garment. Black gloves and a mask of some sort to cover her white face completed the costume. And her familiarity with the room allowed her to move about in silence."

"All well and good," Buckley said, "but the woman was *outside* the locked door, pounding on it, less than a minute after Vargas was stabbed. Explain that."

"Simple misdirection, Mister Buckley. Before the stabbing she replaced all props in the sideboard and closed the top, then unlocked the door . . . the key made a faint scraping and the bolt clicked, sounds which John and I both heard. Then she crossed the room, plunged her dagger into Vargas, recrossed the room immediately after the second thrust, let herself out into the darkened hallway, and relocked the door from that side. Not with Vargas's key, which remained on the sideboard, but with a duplicate key of her own."

No one spoke for a couple of seconds. In hushed tones, then, Grace Cobb asked: "Why did you do it, Annabelle?"

The psychic's mouth twisted. Her voice, when it came, was fiery with passion. "He was an evil unbeliever. He mocked the spirits with his schemes, laughed and derided them and those of us who truly believe. I did his bidding because I loved him, I obeyed him until the spirits came in the night and told me I must obey no longer. They said I must destroy him. Angkar guided my hand tonight. Angkar showed me the path to the truth and light of the after-world. . . ."

Her words trailed off; she sat staring fixedly. Looking at no one there with her blazing eyes, Quincannon thought, but at whoever she believed waited for her beyond the pale.

It was after midnight before the bumbling constabulary (Quincannon considered all city policemen to be bumbling) finished with their questions, took Annabelle away, and permitted the others to depart. On the mist-wet walk in front, while they waited for hansoms, Cyrus Buckley drew Quincannon aside.

"You and Missus Carpenter are competent detectives, sir, I'll grant you that even though I don't wholly approve of your methods. You'll have my check for the balance of our arrangement tomorrow morning."

Quincannon bowed and accepted the financier's hand.

"If you should find yourself in need of our services again. . . ."

"I trust I won't." Buckley paused to unwrap a long-nine cigar. "One question before we part. As I told you in your offices, the first séance Missus Buckley and I attended here was concluded by Vargas's claim that Angkar had untied him. We heard the rope flung through the air, and, when the gas was turned up, we saw it lying unknotted on the floor. He couldn't have untied all those knots himself, with only one free hand."

"Hardly. Annabelle assisted in that trick, too."

"I don't quite see how it was worked. Can you make a guess?"

"I can. The unknotted rope, which he himself hurled across the room, was not the same one with which he was tied. Annabelle slipped up behind him and cut the knotted rope into pieces with her dagger, then hid the pieces in the sideboard. The second rope was concealed there with the props and given to Vargas after she'd severed the first."

"His planned finale for tonight's séance, I fancy."

"No doubt. Instead, Annabelle improvised a far more shocking finish."

"Made him pay dearly for mocking the spirits, eh?"

"If you like, Mister Buckley. If you like."

Quincannon had time to smoke a bowlful of shag tobacco before a hansom arrived for him and Sabina. Settled in the darkened coach on the way to Russian Hill, he said: "All's well that ends well. But I must say I'm glad this case is closed. Psychic phenomena, theocratic unity . . . bah. The lot of it is. . . ."

". . . horsefeathers," Sabina said. "Yes, I know. But are you quite sure there's no truth in it?"

"Spiritualism? None whatsoever."

"Not spiritualism. The existence of a spirit afterlife."

"Don't tell me you give a whit of credence to such folly?"

"I have an open mind."

"So do I, my dear, on most matters."

"But not the paranormal."

"Not a bit of it."

For a time they sat in companionable stillness broken only by the jangle of the horses' bit chains, the clatter of the iron wheels on rough cobblestones. Then there was a faint stirring in the heavy darkness, and to Quincannon's utter amazement, a pair of soft, sweet lips brushed his, clung passionately for an instant, then withdrew.

He sat stunned for several beats. At which point his lusty natural instincts took over; he twisted on the seat, reached out to Sabina with eager hands and mouth. Both found yielding flesh. He kissed her soundly.

In the next second, he found himself embracing a struggling, squirming spitfire. She pulled free, and the crack of her hand on his cheek was twice as hard as the slap in Vargas's spirit room. "What makes you think you can take such liberties, John Quincannon?" she demanded indignantly.

"But . . . I was only returning your affection. . . ."

"*My* affection?"

"You kissed me first. Why, if you didn't care to have it reciprocated?"

"What are you gabbling about? I didn't kiss you."

"Of course you did. A few moments ago."

"*Faugh!* I did no such thing and you know it." Her dress rustled as she slid farther away from him. "Now, I'll thank you to keep your distance and behave yourself."

He sat and behaved, not happily. Had he imagined the

kiss? No, he wasn't that moonstruck. She had kissed him, for a fact; he could still feel her lips against his. Some sort of woman's game to devil him. He imagined her smiling secretly in the dark—but then the hack passed close to a street lamp, and he saw that she was leaning against the far door with her arms folded, unsmiling and wearing an injured look.

The only other explanation for the kiss . . . but that was sheer lunacy, not worth a moment's consideration. It must have been Sabina. Of course it was Sabina. And yet. . . .

The hansom clattered on into the cold, damp night.

Quincannon in Paradise

I

It took Quincannon more than an hour to find the shabby bungalow on the lower slope of Punchbowl Hill. The streets had been laid out in a confusing hodge-podge and that rattlepate Fenner's directions left much to be desired. He was in a wicked humor when he finally located Hoapili Street and the right house half hidden behind tall hibiscus shrubs and stubby palms. He parked the hired buggy in the shade of a thorny *kiawe* tree, wiped his dripping face with an already soggy handkerchief. His thick beard itched. His lightweight tropical clothing felt as wet and clammy as if he had been doused with a bucket of water. Even the grip of his Navy Colt seemed to be sweating when he touched it.

Lonesome Jack Vereen and the Nevada Kid had best not give him any trouble when he braced them, he thought darkly. If they resisted, the consequences would be on their heads.

He paused to reconnoiter before he left the buggy's side. Two other bungalows were within sight, these also roofed with palm-leaf thatch and surrounded by jungly vegetation. There was no sign of life anywhere except for a scruffy mongrel dog panting in the shade across the road. The late afternoon was breathlessly still. His quarries were both night creatures, like the vampires of legend; at this hour they likely would be asleep, or at least half comatose with heat and drink. Both were dedicated carousers. Fenner had told him that the pair had been seen locally in the company of an island rancher named Millay, who was evidently a fellow roisterer—the three of them ruining their gizzards with large quantities of *okolehao*, a potent Hawaiian liquor distilled from the roots of *ti* plants. Nevertheless, like all criminals they presented a potential danger when cornered. It would behoove him to proceed slowly and cautiously and to take them by surprise—not that he intended to move otherwise in this blasted tropical furnace.

He adjusted the Navy's holster until it rode more comfortably on his hip. Then he set off down the road, keeping to pockets of shadow wherever possible. The line of hibiscus along the rear side of the bungalow afforded enough cover so that he was able to approach it on a more or less straight trajectory. When he reached the shrubs, he moved along parallel to them, through tall grass, until he came to a point where the sweet-flowered tangle grew thinly enough for him to see through. Unrolled blinds covered a single window in the side wall. Along the front, part of a rickety, overgrown verandah was visible. He stood listening. The stillness remained unbroken.

Stealthily he made his way around to the rear, past the bushes to where a privy leaned and a grove of mango trees overpowered the hibiscus with the odor of overripe fruit. The back entrance had two doors, the outer one screened against insects and the inner one open for ventilation. Quincannon allowed a brief, feral grin to split his freebooter's beard. He drew the Navy, walked softly across a patch of grass to the screened door.

It was not latched. He eased it open an inch or two; the hinges made no sound. He widened the gap just enough to edge his big body through, let the door whisper shut again behind him.

He was in a small kitchen all but filled by a table and chairs and a cast-iron stove. The table and the stove top were littered with unwashed dishes and food remnants a-crawl with insects; the two grifters were of the type who kept themselves tidy while permitting their surroundings to descend into chaos. From there, Quincannon surveyed the empty and equally disarrayed room beyond. Another doorway stood at his left, this one covered with a bead curtain. It would lead to the bedroom, the only other room in a dwelling of this size.

Trapped heat made the place a sweatbox; his face and body were dripping again as he drifted across the room. Another smell came to him then, one far less pleasant than those outside. He knew that one all too well. Hell and damn! There was no longer any need for stealth. He shouldered through the curtain, causing the beads to click violently.

Two narrow bamboo-framed daybeds were braced against opposite walls. One had nothing on it but a soiled blanket. The dead man was sprawled on his back across the other, fully dressed, mouth and eyes open wide; the black-dried blood on his shirtfront had become a meal for flies and ants. Shot twice at close range, from the look of the wounds. Sometime yesterday, he judged.

Exit the Nevada Kid.

Quincannon holstered his weapon, breathing through his mouth, and went to the bed. The Kid's trouser pockets contained a gold pocket watch, the inside lid inscribed **To Harold from His Loving Wife**—the Kid's real name had been Benjamin Joplin and he had never been married—a coin purse, a Barlow knife, and several pieces of hard candy. The shirt pocket was empty. The frock coat, much too heavy for this climate, was draped over a chair at the foot of the bed. Its pockets yielded a packet of lucifers, a long-nine stogy, and two well-pawed French postcards that Quincannon studied judiciously before replacing.

As he was about to re-drape the coat, his fingers encountered something that crinkled in the lining of one of the tails. An examination of the lining revealed a hidden pocket containing a folded piece of paper—a map, crudely drawn in India ink by an unsteady hand. This appeared to be an outline of an island with an irregular coastline. One of the Hawaiian islands, likely. It was not named, but printed in a crabbed hand along the left-hand edge were several labeled Xs: Kawaihae, Puako, Auohe, Waimae Pt., Kailua. The X that bore the name Auohe was heavily inked and circled.

Quincannon pocketed the map. He found nothing else of interest there, nor in the front room. Glowering, he left the bungalow as he'd entered it and made his way back along the deserted road to where he had parked the buggy.

The glower held fast during the drive back to the city center. An affront, that was what this investigation had become. A personal affront. And he was not about to stand for it.

He was, after all, the finest, cleverest detective in the United States, if not in the entire world. A relentless manhunter with a brilliantly deductive mind. He had chased down miscreants the length and breadth of California, across a dozen states and territories. Few had escaped him, none that he would admit to publicly. He would, as he was fond of declaiming, pursue a quarry to the ends of the earth, even into the bowels of the Pit if necessary.

The one place he'd never considered was paradise.

Not true paradise, of course, in which he would surely spend eternity despite his not altogether virtuous history. But until this case, even an earthly paradise, or what was widely considered to be one, had seemed an unlikely spot for one of his tenacious manhunts. When the opportunity to come here had presented itself, he had been pleased at the prospect. It presented a challenge to his skills, meant a fat fee to swell the coffers of Carpenter and Quincannon, Professional Detective Services, and promised both new vistas and fresh benefits. "Think of the publicity," he had said to Sabina. "Every newspaper within two hundred miles will print the story of John Quincannon's three-thousand-mile quest for justice. Our reputations will soar, we'll reap a harvest of new clients. . . ."

"That's all well and good," she said, "if you can find that pair of swindlers and recover Mister Anderson's property."

"Have I failed us yet, my dear?"

"Not lately. But they've eluded you for two months already, and they've done so in familiar territory. You'll be operating in a strange new world, John."

"Strange to them, too, don't forget."

"Still. There's a first time for everything, including a three-thousand-mile failure."

He paid no attention to this defeatist talk. He was supremely confident, as always. Lonesome Jack Vereen and the Nevada Kid may have managed to elude him in Oakland, San Jose, and San Francisco, but that was purely a matter of faulty timing and bad luck. He'd dealt with grifters and thimble-riggers before, on several occasions; cunning gents when it came to such trickery as three-card monte, the gold-brick and green-goods games, or the stock swindle they had perpetrated on Mr. R. W. Anderson of Oakland, but also spendthrifts and habitual gamblers and womanizers—traits that made them easy prey for a seasoned manhunter. True, he had yet to discover why they had booked passage three days ahead of him on a steamship bound for the Hawaiian Islands—likely they'd tumbled on a new mark for one of the confidence games—but once arrived in Honolulu they were sure to frequent the same type of fleshpots as they had in California. They would not be difficult to find.

Ah, the Hawaiian Islands. Eight of them grouped together in the Pacific Ocean, where lush tropical vegetation grew in thick profusion and the sky was a soft blue and balmy trade winds wafted gently over white sand beaches and the Polynesian natives all wore friendly smiles and sun-browned girls performed exotic dances clad in little more than flower *leis*. Dubbed paradise by all who'd been there, including such luminaries as Robert Louis Stevenson and Mark Twain. A relatively short and restful ocean voyage, on a ship renowned for its sumptuous cuisine; two or three days to locate the humbuggers and confiscate the stocks and what remained of the cash they'd filched from R. W. Anderson; a week or so in which to partake of the various pleasures paradise had to offer (at least one of which he would not discuss with Sabina), and then another relaxing sea voyage and home again to his partner's adulation and the promise of more fat fees.

So he'd thought upon sailing through the Golden Gate.

But not for long.

Restful ocean voyage, sumptuous cuisine? There were storms and rough seas six of the seven days' passage, and he'd neither left his cabin until the ship steamed into Honolulu harbor nor was able to eat anything other than milk-soaked bread and oatmeal the entire time. He had never been sicker or spent a more miserable week in his life.

Soft blue sky, balmy trade winds? The heavens were seared white with a sticky, sweltering heat, the lush tropical vegetation hung, limp and lifeless. The simple act of drawing breath made sweat flow from the pores. Kona season, the clerk at his hotel informed him apologetically. The kind of weather that brewed storms and volcanic eruptions, produced restlessness and irritability in locals as well as tourists, and was believed by native Polynesians to be "dying weather".

Smiling natives? Exotic dances performed by half-naked girls? Few of the islanders he'd encountered had bared their teeth except in panting scowls, fewer still had exhibited friendly behavior, and a couple of scruffy types had studied his neck as if measuring it for a noose or a knife blade. And all the young women wore charms-covering sarongs or missionary-induced Mother Hubbards and showed no inclination to dance or perform any other exotic activity that required energetic movement.

Two or three days to track down and arrest his quarry and confiscate the spoils? It had taken him less than two days, as a matter of fact, with the help of James Q. Fenner and his local contacts, to locate the Hoapili Street bungalow—the only positive note in the entire trip thus far. But now he couldn't arrest either of the grifters because the Nevada Kid was lying dead with two bullets in his black heart and there was no indication of the whereabouts of Lonesome Jack Vereen or the valuables stolen from R. W. Anderson.

Paradise?

Bah!

Merchant Street, a block from the docks, was a narrow avenue flanked by heavy, square buildings built of stone that had been brought to the islands in the holds of New England windjammers. The center of the city's commerce, it was also the location for the Honolulu Police Station. Quincannon, on foot after returning the rented buggy to the livery, walked past the imposing structure without slowing. He continued beneath the arcades of counting-houses and the Inter-Island Steamship Building, at a plodding gait in deference to the oppressive heat. Few others were abroad, and the cobblestone street was mostly empty of carriages.

At the head of Merchant Street, he crossed over into Nuuanu Avenue. There was more activity here, mainly supplied by sailors of several nationalities on the prowl for women and women on the prowl for sailors. Nuuanu was called Fid Street by the locals, Fenner had informed him, a reference to the seafarer's term for grog; it was Honolulu's version of the Barbary Coast, a small but potent section that had earned the city its reputation among sailors as a "Port of Hell". Bagnios proliferated here, as did saloons bearing such names as Red Lion, Ship and Whale, South Sea Taps, and spewing forth a great deal of noise, laughter, and bawdy talk. The atmosphere and Babel were a taste of home to Quincannon.

Next door to a boisterous deadfall humorously called Hanrahan's Rest was a two-story clapboard building that housed a sailors' outfitter downstairs and Fenner's office upstairs. It was a poor location for a detective agency, but Fenner was willing to forego a client or two in exchange for its proximity to Hanrahan's. He had a vast fondness and capacity for beer and owned up to making three or four daily treks next door for a fresh bucket. If he'd been able to convince or coerce the outfitter to move elsewhere, so he could take over the ground floor space, he would have been a contented man. But the outfitter was stubborn and refused to leave, and because Fenner was too niggardly to hire a runner, he was forced to climb up and down the outside stairs himself several times a day. This made him shorttempered. The Kona season had further blackened his disposition. The sweltering humidity gave him rashes, he said, and not even an extra bucket or two of lager provided him with relief.

For all of his shortcomings, Fenner was a competent fly cop. Until three years ago he had been a member of the Honolulu constabulary, under the authority of the Marshal of the Kingdom of Hawaii. Quincannon had first met him in this capacity in 1891, during his stint as an operative of the United States Secret Service; Fenner had come to San Francisco as a security officer in the entourage accompanying Kalakaua, the last king of Hawai'i, who had eventually died in the city. In January of 1893 the Hawaiian Kingdom had breathed its last as well. Fenner had supported Marshal Charles B. Wilson in refusing for several hours to turn over the police station to the new provisional government, and this had cost him his job and led him reluctantly to open his own investigative service.

He bulked hugely behind his desk, like a scowling Caucasian Buddha, when Quincannon entered the office. Raisin-like eyes nestled in fat pouches regarded him with surprise. "What, back so soon? Those two *kolohe* not at the house?"

"One of them was."

"Well? Didn't you put him in handcuffs?"

"Not much point in handcuffing a dead man," Quincannon said.

"What's that? Dead?"

"The Nevada Kid. Shot twice and ripening in the heat."

"How long ago?"

"Sometime yesterday."

"And no sign of the other one?"

"Not a trace. No luggage, nothing left behind but his partner's corpse."

Fenner mopped his red face with a bandanna-size handkerchief, then quaffed deeply from a cocoanut shell mug of beer. "You haven't reported this to the police, I take it?"

"No, and I've no intention of doing so."

"I thought not."

"Lonesome Jack Vereen is my game. No one is going to arrest him or shoot him but John Quincannon."

Fenner essayed a grin beneath his brushy mustaches. "You're a man after my own heart, Quincannon," he said. "Smart, hard, and unscrupulous when the situation warrants. That's why I like you. Even if you have become a temperance man."

Quincannon allowed as how he liked himself for the same reasons. And that he was hardly a temperance man; he held no brief against either demon rum or beer; his reasons for no longer imbibing were strictly personal.

"I never fault a man for his personal beliefs," Fenner said. He drank again, thirstily. "Why do you suppose Vereen shot his partner? A falling out of some sort?"

"Possibly. The pair had no long-term friendship, merely a grifters' relationship of short duration. But the spoils from the Anderson swindle weren't large enough to trigger mayhem. More likely, whatever brought the pair to Hawaii is responsible."

"Another swindle?"

"With a much larger cush than they're used to playing for."

Fenner said musingly: "George Millay would make a fine mark."

"Would he now?"

"Millay and his sister Grace own a large ranch on the Big Island. She runs it. He spends much of the profits, and none too careful how."

"Wastrel?"

"Blow-hard, tosspot, and rakehell is more like it. Women, *okolehao*, games of chance. One of those harum-scarum sports long on wind and short on common sense."

"Just the sort to attract the likes of Lonesome Jack and the Kid. What kind of ranch is it?"

"Cattle. Prime beef."

"A cattle ranch? In Hawaii?"

"Several large ranches over there. The largest by a wide margin is the Parker Ranch . . . they run more than fifty thousand head. The Millays' ranks fourth or fifth, I'm not sure which."

"Fifty thousand head?" Quincannon was astonished.

"Thriving cattle business in the islands," Fenner told him. "Has been for nearly a hundred years."

Quincannon fished out the crude map he'd taken from the Nevada Kid's coat and laid it on the desk. "Would this by any chance be a drawing of the Big Island?"

Fenner gave it a quick study, quaffing again from his cocoanut shell mug as he did so. "It would," he said. "Kailua is the largest town on the Kona coast. Kawaihae and Puako . . . little fishing villages, if I remember right. It's been years since my last visit to that part of the Big Island."

"Is the Millay Ranch located there?"

"Inland between Puako and Waimae Point, I think. On the lower slopes of Mauna Kea."

"And *Auohe?*"

"A Hawaiian word that means 'hidden place'. As far as I know, there's no village or anything else along that stretch of coast that carries the name."

"You've no idea what it might refer to on this map?"

"None. Unless it marks the location of the ranch road, but I don't see how that would translate to *auohe*."

"Mayhap the gent who brokered the Hoapili Street bungalow has the answer. His name again?"

"Justo Gomez. But I doubt they'd have confided in the likes of him."

"I'll ask him nonetheless. Where does he hang his hat?"

"On the waterfront. Justo's Bait and Tackle Shop . . . a cover for his shadier enterprises."

Quincannon stood up. Even that much activity in the stifling, airless office caused his breath to come short. His mouth and throat felt parched; he watched Fenner have at his suds with the first twinge of envy since he'd taken the pledge years ago. "How long is this blasted heat expected to last?"

"Not much longer. It never lasts more than a week or two this time of year. The Kona winds are actually blownout typhoons that've come up across the equator and they bring plenty of rain along with 'em. There'll be a hell of a howling storm tonight and tomorrow."

Quincannon said—"Another delightful day in paradise."—and went out muttering to himself.

III

The ships anchored in Honolulu harbor sat motionless on the gun-metal gray water, as if they had been carved from gigantic blocks of wood. The sky, which seemed to have been flattened down over the sea beyond the breakwater, had a milky, shimmering radiance that burned the eye. Kanaka stevedores moved sluggishly on the docks, loading and unloading cargo at a retarded pace that would have cost them their pay on San Francisco's Embarcadero. Even the dray horses stood or plodded limply in the sodden heat.

Quincannon felt as if he were melting by the time he dragged himself into Justo's Bait and Tackle Shop. The torrid weather had given his thoughts a fuzzy dullness, but his temper was still crimped and primed. Anything was liable to set it off, including even a whisper of uncooperation.

The shop was small and ramshackle and smelled heavily of brine and spoiled fish. Nets hung dustily from two bare walls. Behind a plank laid across a pair of sawhorses, a man clad only in dungarees sat sprawled in a rattan chair with his feet up on the plank. He was short and wiry, dark-skinned, with black hair and black eyes and features that proclaimed his Portuguese/Hawaiian ancestry. Sweat glistened on his naked chest and arms like oil on burnished wood.

Only the black eyes moved as Quincannon approached him. They were shrewd, measuring. After a few seconds of scrutiny, his mouth opened over as many gold teeth as white in a wily grin.

"*Aloha,*" he said.

"Justo Gomez?"

"Sure, that's me." The grin widened. "Man, you look like you just off some pirate ship. What's your name?"

"Quincannon."

"That brush you got on your face, somebody ever call you Blackbeard?"

"None that ever lived to draw another breath."

Gomez lost his grin. He swung his feet off the plank, stood up slowly. "What you want, *haole?* Somebody looks like you, dressed like you ain't interested in fishing."

"I'm looking for Jack Vereen."

"Who?"

"Lonesome Jack Vereen."

"Never heard of somebody with that name."

"*Bah.* A few days ago you rented him and Ben Joplin, the Nevada Kid, a bungalow on Hoapili Street. Vereen moved out yesterday."

"What you telling me this story for? I don't know you, I don't know nothing about those other *haoles.*"

"The Kid's still there," Quincannon said. "Dead. Shot twice through the heart."

Gomez possessed a gambler's countenance. His only reaction was a squint in one eye. "That ain't trouble for me," he said.

"No? It's your bungalow."

"I don't own no property 'cept this shop. Somebody shot dead, that somebody else's *pilikia.*"

"Where can I find Jack Vereen?"

"You come to the wrong place for finding somebody," Gomez said, and shrugged. "Justo sells bait, nets to catch fish. He don't sell information."

"But you'll give it of your own free will."

"You crazy in the head if that's what you think. . . ."

Quincannon made a swift draw of his Colt. At the same

time, with his other hand, he reached across the plank and took a firm grip on Gomez's ear. He drew the man's head forward, and then inserted the Navy's muzzle in the opposite ear. Gomez squawked like a frightened parrot. He struggled briefly, stopped struggling when Quincannon applied pressure.

"In my twenty years as a detective I've killed fourteen men," he lied, "including two who withheld vital information from me. I won't lose any sleep tonight if you're number fifteen."

There was a pregnant silence.

"Lonesome Jack Vereen," Quincannon said. "You have five seconds, Justo."

It took only two for Gomez to say: "Gone."

"Gone where?"

"Big Island." The liquid voice had an odd scratchy sound now, as if Gomez's vocal chords had acquired a coat of rust.

"When did he leave?"

"Yesterday."

"Did you arrange passage for him?"

"No. He gone on inter-island boat to Hilo and Kailua."

"Why?"

"I don't know."

Quincannon screwed the Navy's muzzle another quarter inch into his ear canal.

"Man, I don't know!" Gomez said promptly. "He got some kine deal with rich *haole* own big ranch over there."

"George Millay."

"You know him, hah?"

"Do *you* know him?"

"Poor bait seller like Justo don't know no rich *haoles*."

"What kind of deal does Vereen have with George Millay?"

"Don't know. Him and his partner, they don't tell me nothing."

"Then how do you know there is a deal?"

"Hear about it. Friends, they listen, tell me things."

"Any friend in particular?"

"Plenty people see them together about every night since they come in from mainland."

"What was George Millay doing in San Francisco?"

"Buy cattle, sell cattle. Maybe raise plenty hell on Barbary Coast."

"Why did he spend the last three nights in Honolulu? More sport?"

"Sure. Raise hell here, like always. Got cattle business, too, maybe."

"And he left yesterday bound for home. With Vereen."

"Sure, both of them. Gone."

Quincannon removed the barrel and released the other ear. Gomez backed off quickly, rubbing both sides of his head. His glare was a mixture of pain, fear, and malevolence.

"You some bad kine fella," he said, not without respect. "What you gonna do to that Vereen when you catch him? Number fifteen?"

"And you'll be number sixteen if you try to get in my way."

"Poor Justo," Gomez said mournfully. He'd decided to feel sorry for himself. "Always got *pilikia nui*. Wife, six children, police, now bad kine fella like you."

Quincannon went out into the breathless afternoon, made his slow way back to Merchant Street and the Inter-Island Steamship Company. The next ship leaving for the

Big Island wasn't scheduled until the morning; he booked cabin passage to Kailua, some thirty to forty miles from the South Kohala cattle ranches.

That evening he spent in making the rounds of the Nuuanu Avenue deadfalls, seeking more information on the relationship between George Millay and the two confidence grifters. He found little other than the fact that the three men had spent most of their evenings in Honolulu's most notorious sporting house, the Bird of Paradise, where the pleasures were rumored to be amazingly exotic and expensive. He considered a visit there himself, in a strictly professional capacity, of course, and might have given in to the impulse if it hadn't been for the devil's weather. It was too damned hot to engage in any strenuous activity.

Limp and weary, he returned to his hotel. The heat followed him into his room and robbed him of sleep. Later, past midnight, so did the promised storm—a hellish thing full of howling winds and slashing blades of lightning and a continuing onslaught of rain.

IV

The storm cooled the night somewhat, but as soon as the worst of it had passed, the temperature rose again and humidity re-choked the air. By morning it was every bit as sultry as the day before. Quincannon knew without being told that more Kona storms were in the offing. He could only maintain the dismal hope that the next would hold off until he had completed his passage to the Big Island.

It didn't, curse his luck. It struck when the little inter-island steamer *Island Princess* was an hour out from Honolulu harbor, not quite as powerful as the one during the night but strong enough to boil the sea and toss the ship around like a toy and play havoc with Quincannon's tender stomach.

This storm blew itself out shortly before the ship reached Hilo. Quincannon emerged, shaken and wobbly, as they drew into the harbor. The offshore wind that greeted him was softer, cooler, scented with tropical sweetness, but it did nothing to improve either his physical or mental well-being. He leaned on the railing, staring up at the looming presence of one of the island's volcanoes, this one called Mauna Loa, and the small port settlement that stretched out beyond a long expanse of palm-fringed white beach.

The wharf at which the steamer docked looked new, as did some of the rows of warehouses along the waterfront. The town buildings and houses were a mixture of old and new, a few made of stone, more of unpainted timber, more still of woven palm fronds with thatched roofs. Quincannon regarded Hilo with a covetous eye. It was not a particularly inviting place, but it had one attribute that made him yearn to be disembarking here: it sprawled across solid ground.

The *Island Princess*'s lay-over was short. Most of the passengers disembarked here, a handful took their place, cargo was quickly loaded and off-loaded, and they were soon under way again. The ocean on the leeward side of the island was considerably calmer, permitting Quincannon to remain on deck throughout the voyage to the Kona Coast. The brisk sea wind cooled him; his tortured insides eased. When they drew off Kailua, he felt more or less his old self.

The village was a straggling affair of thirty or forty buildings that hugged the shore beside a protected bay. The dominant structure, Quincannon was informed by one of the passengers, was a royal palace built by Prince Kuakini, brother of Kamehameha's queen. To his jaundiced eye, it looked less like a palace than a square, three-storied New England house onto which had been grafted a long porch and a second-story balcony with ornate railings. A massive banyan tree embraced it; coconut palms and an explosion of tropical blooms shaded the porch.

Quincannon noted all of this as he off-loaded himself and his carpetbag, first onto the slender dock and then onto blessed earth. He trudged to a small hotel that the steamer's steward had pointed out to him. The weather was not as hot here, although the afternoon still felt sultry. But the sky was heavy with restless clouds that promised another tempest by nightfall.

The hotel accommodations were Spartan but adequate. The owner was a Caucasian named Abner Bannister, a slat of a man with a bristling mustache who proudly proclaimed himself the descendant of one of the missionaries who had helped Prince Kuakini design his royal home in 1837. Quincannon allowed as how he was there on a business matter concerning George Millay, and asked if Millay and a companion had stopped here within the past two days. The answer was no, although Bannister had been informed of their arrival; the pair had evidently gone straight on to the ranch.

"How far is the Millay Ranch from here?" Quincannon asked him.

"About thirty miles, as the crow flies."

"Would it be possible to hire a boat to take me to the nearest village?"

"The only boats in Kailua are fisherman's outriggers. And there are no passenger boats to Puako. Of course, one of the cattle ships from Hilo could take you to Kawaihae. They anchor offshore there, you know, when ranchers drive their herds to the beach. The cattle are lashed to the outside of small boats and ferried out to the main ship where they're belly-hoisted aboard. . . ."

"Is a cattle boat due soon?" Quincannon interrupted.

"No, not for another two weeks."

"There is a road, I take it?"

"Oh, yes. Quite a good one by island standards."

"Where can I rent a horse?"

Bannister laughed. "There are no horses for hire in Kailua. The *lios* in this district have either been domesticated for use on the ranches and plantations, or roam wild."

"How do people make the trip, then? By shank's mare?"

"No, no, there are wagons. And Kona Nightingales."

". . . What, pray tell, is a Kona Nightingale?"

"An island breed of donkey. Durable and sturdy creatures, for the most part quite dependable when domesticated."

Donkeys! No boats, no horses, naught but wagons and asses! *Faugh!* One blasted indignity after another.

Bannister sent one of his Hawaiian employees to make transportation arrangements for the following morning, saving Quincannon at least that disagreeable task. After a roast pork supper, palatable save for a strange paste-like side dish called *poi,* the two men retired to the hotel parlor to smoke their pipes. If there were any other guests in the hotel, they had not made themselves visible in the dining room or anywhere else on the premises. Bannister was the loquacious type, and willing to share confidences. He was also, it developed, something of a local historian.

Quincannon asked him about the Millay Ranch, stating that he knew relatively little of its operation or of the family; his business with the Millays was of a highly sensitive and private nature. The hotel owner accepted this without question.

"It's one of the larger ranches in South Kohala," Bannister said. "Several thousand acres extending from the lower slopes of Mauna Kea to the sea. And several thousand head of cattle. Grace and George's father, Glendon Millay, was deeded the land by Queen Kapiolani at the behest of John Parker, the owner of the largest ranch on the island. Parker was an intimate of King Kamehameha and the first to domesticate the wild herds of longhorns brought to the island in 1793, and Glendon Millay was one of his employees. Hawaiian longhorns are small and wiry, you know, not like the Texas variety. . . ."

Quincannon cut this short by saying: "I understand Grace Millay is the guiding force behind the ranch today."

"Ever since Glendon's death eight years ago, yes. With the help of a dozen or so *paniolos* and her *luna,* Sam Opaka."

"*Luna?*"

"Ranch foreman. Rough sort, half-caste. There are rumors, of course, but I for one pay no attention to them. Gossip is a tool of the devil."

Yes, and of a detective on the hunt. "Rumors about Grace Millay and Sam Opaka, do you mean?"

"Sadly, yes. Neither is married and they are often seen together, and so the inevitable conclusions are drawn." Bannister sighed. "Grace is a handsome woman. Most handsome. But, ah, willful and tenacious, if you know what I mean."

"Indeed." If any man understood forceful women, it was John Quincannon. The description was one he himself might have used to signify Sabina. "And her brother? He has no objection to her running the ranch?"

"None. He prefers it. He's . . . less tenacious, shall we say, than his sister. Younger by five years, just twenty-seven. He prefers the buying and selling end of the business."

"I've been told he travels extensively and is known as quite a sport."

"*Ahem.* Yes, well, he has that reputation."

"This may seem like an odd question, but I have my reasons for asking it. Do you know of any spot on that part of the coast that might be referred to as *auohe?*"

"Hidden place? Well," Bannister said, "let me think. There isn't much along that part of the coastline except volcanic rock, black sand beaches, and a *kiawe* forest to the east. But there are numerous caves and lava tubes, some quite large and reputed to extend for miles. Is that what you mean?"

"Possibly. What exactly is a lava tube?"

"Just what the name implies. Tubes formed centuries ago when molten flows from Mauna Kea cooled and hardened as they neared the sea and new flows tunneled through. Legend has it that there are undiscovered burial chambers in tubes along the Kohala coast."

"Burial chambers?"

"It was the custom of the ancient kings and those of royal blood to have their clothing and other possessions interred with their remains. The locations were kept secret for privacy reasons. . . . Ah! That reminds me. Just south of the Millay Ranch road, near Waimae Point, there is an inlet where an old *heiau* once stood. I suppose it might be considered a hidden place."

"And what is a *heiau?*"

"A Hawaiian temple," Bannister said. "After a volcanic eruption destroyed part of the low cliffs there long ago, a *kahunapule* . . . a high priest . . . ordered a temple built on the site. Grass huts that housed various wooden idols, stone altar platforms where sacrifices were offered to the gods. The early missionaries had the huts and idols burned. No one goes to the ruins."

"No? Why is that?"

"Natives are superstitious and *heiaus* were forbidden, taboo. The ruins can also be dangerous at high tide. The rocks there are unstable and there is rather a large *puka* in the ledge there. Blowhole, you know."

Quincannon let the conversation lapse. Danger was his life's blood. And if there was anything hidden among the *heiau*'s ruins, he would find it.

V

He left Kailua shortly past dawn the next morning. It had stormed again during the night, but at this hour the sky was mostly clear and the offshore wind comfortably warm. Only the ever-present humid stickiness suggested another blistering day ahead. The hired wagon was little more than a wooden cart with iron wheels, but its bed was large enough to hold a trussed prisoner on the return trip; now it contained only his carpetbag and a basket of food provided by Abner Bannister. As for the creature in the traces, he had never seen one quite like it. It was smaller than the asses he was used to, and resembled nothing so much as a leathery-skinned mouse grown to fifty times its normal size. He had eyed it skeptically on first encounter; it seemed incapable of either the stamina for a thirty-mile trip or the ability to move along at any but a retarded speed. The impression, at least in the early stages of the trek, had proved false. The animal trotted along the muddy, rutted road with no evident strain and at a steady pace.

Kailua lay in lowlands dominated by vast plantations of coffee and sugar cane. The road ran on a more or less level grade through the fields, then began to skirt the edges of inland hills grayed by volcanic ash. Ancient lava flows from Mauna Kea had permanently scarred the landscape, leaving humped, blackened rocks to mark their path to the sea. The volcano loomed high to the east, its snow-covered crest sheathed and mostly hidden by clouds.

By nine o'clock the heat had gathered and begun to lay heavy on Quincannon's head and shoulders. He donned the planter's hat Bannister had provided for a nominal fee, took frequent sips from a water bottle. He stopped once to give the Kona Nightingale a drink and a bait of grain, using his hat for a bowl; otherwise the donkey plodded along without apparent need for rest.

Shortly past eleven by his stem-winder they crested a hill, from where he could see a considerable distance along the rugged coast. Huge blackened lava swaths cut through the greens and browns; some of the beaches were of black sand, an oddly unreal sight in their fringes of coconut palms. Where the road descended near one of these, he stopped again and sought shade under one of the palms in which to partake of the sandwiches and fruit Bannister had packed for him.

The day wore on. Mile after mile jolted away. He passed a hamlet of grass shacks and a handful of wagons driven by native Hawaiians, saw no one else. Sun flame and the dusty, sultry air turned his disposition as black and bleak as the lava scars. There would come a day when he would look back on this adventure as an example of the ends to which a great manhunter would go to bring his quarry to justice, and regale Sabina with descriptions of his many tropical hardships. But that day was far off.

He reached the old temple in early afternoon, although he would not have recognized it as such if it hadn't been for a pair of landmarks provided by Abner Bannister—a stunted kukui tree growing atilt between two spire-like rocks and the arrowhead-shaped ledge jutting out into the sea. There may have been cliffs here at one time, but molten lava had flattened them down into a long, wide slope ridged and humped and strewn with huge boulders. From the road he could see the blowhole in the ledge's outer end, and below that a sandy beach neither black nor white but a dark gray. A strong offshore wind blew here and the sea had roughened; tidewater mixed with air boiled into the seaward end of what Bannister had described as a funnel-like tube beneath the ledge, and sent spray geysering 100 feet into the air. The falling water drenched the rocks there and made them glisten like black glass.

Quincannon tied the donkey to the kukui tree. An ancient trail leading down to the temple was nearby, but it took him a while to find it. The descent was gradual, but the sharp-edged lava rock made for poor footing and slow progress. As he neared the ledge, the roar and gurgle of the spouting blowhole was thunderous. A flattish, inland extension of the ledge led in among the overhanging rocks. There, hidden from the road, was where he found the ruins of the *heiau*.

All that remained standing were sections of the outer walls. Forbidden entry, Bannister had told him. *Bah.* Ancient superstitions meant nothing to Quincannon, or nothing to which he would admit in the light of day. He found a passage between two of the sections, followed it into an open expanse some fifty rods in diameter. The floor was uneven, littered with sharp rocks. Flat volcanic slabs, cracked and broken, were arranged at its rear—the ancient sacrificial stones. There was no sign of the huts or idols that had once been displayed here.

He prowled the *heiau* for a time, finding nothing to have inspired the crude map or the murder of the Nevada Kid. There were several narrow, tight-fitting openings into the maze of rocks, one or more of which might have been man-made, but attempting to explore them with no more than a packet of lucifers was a fool's errand. He would need a lantern or a supply of candles for that chore. And it might not be necessary. Wouldn't be if he could get his hands on Lonesome Jack Vereen without incident at the Millay Ranch.

He climbed back up to the road, gigged the Kona Nightingale into a fresh trot. It was a short distance to where the ranch road, marked by a weathered sign and a track worn smooth by countless wheels and hoofs, wound upward through a desolate landscape toward the brooding presence of the volcano. The ascent was sharp and steady, curling through lava beds where the wagon's wheels churned up a black powdery grit that clogged Quincannon's nostrils and streaked his sweating face. Then it passed through the *kiawe* forest, a long jungly stretch in which the trees, none more than a dozen feet in height, were so closely packed that their bare, thorn-laden branches had interlocked to form an impassable tangle on both sides of the road.

Once he emerged from the forest, the grasslands began. The wind that blew at this higher elevation was cooler by several degrees and carried the smell of grass and mountain instead of the sea. Quincannon's spirits rose. The lethargy produced by the long, hot ride began to give way.

Eventually the road debouched into a small, verdant valley. The pastureland here was spotted with longhorn cattle, lean and somewhat stunted by comparison to the burly beeves raised on mainland ranches. At the far end, set into a half circle of trees, he spied the ranch buildings. He sat more erect on the hard seat, smiling thinly in anticipation. The prospect of action always had a limbering effect on his liver.

The ranch house, he saw as he drew near, was a long, low structure of native lumber with hand-squared log walls and a palm-thatch roof, its porch, open on three sides, green-shadowed by the branches of a huge monkey-pod tree. The visible windows had glass panes that caught the lowering rays of the sun and threw back a fiery dazzle. A corral made of thick bamboo poles stretched behind the house. Several outbuildings were also visible, among them stable, dairy barn, and what was likely a bunkhouse for the hands.

Two rough-garbed Hawaiian cowboys were working a pair of horses inside the corral, both animals small and wiry like Indian mustangs and marked with white pinto splotches. Another *paniolo* stood inside the open doors to a blacksmith's shop next to the stable, using a pair of heavy nippers on another horse's hoof. There was no sign of anyone at the main house.

Quincannon drew up at the far end of the yard, nearer the stable. The two *paniolos* in the corral stopped their work and came over to stand silently watching from the fence. The one in the smithy looked up but didn't lower either the nippers or his animal's hoof as Quincannon approached him.

The cowhand was middle-aged, sinewy, with an expressionless face sunburned to the hue of old mahogany. Quincannon stopped at a sidewise angle in the doorway so that he could see the corral and house beyond.

"*Aloha,*" he said. This seemed to be the standard islands

greeting. "You wouldn't be the *luna,* by any chance? Sam Opaka?"

"No. You want Sam?"

"My business is with Jack Vereen."

The name produced no reaction. The *paniolo* finished cutting away heavy cartilage, then picked up a wood rasp to smooth the edges and keep the hoof from splitting. "Don't know him."

"George Millay's friend from the mainland. Just arrived."

"Mister Millay got no *haole* friend here."

"No? Mister Millay is here, isn't he?"

"Come back yesterday. Away long time."

"Are you saying he came back alone?"

"Alone. Sure."

Quincannon stared at him. What the devil was this, now? A lie or evasion, for some reason? If it was the truth, where was Lonesome Jack Vereen?

VI

Scowling, he asked: "Where would I find Mister Millay?"

"Main house, maybe."

"And his sister?"

"She out riding with Sam Opaka. Back pretty soon now."

Quincannon left him to his chore and crossed the yard to the ranch house. It was almost cool in the shade of the monkey-pod. The front door stood open behind a fly-screen; he knocked on the screen's frame. When this produced no response, he used the heel of his hand to make a louder summons.

A voice from the gloom within called out thickly: "Mele! See who that is!"

Quincannon waited. After a minute, when no one appeared, he pounded on the frame again.

"Mele!" Then: "Dammit, who's making all that racket out there?"

"George Millay?"

". . . I don't want to see anybody. Go away."

Quincannon did the opposite: he opened the screen and stepped inside. Once his eyes grew accustomed to the half light, he saw that he was in a large room whose rough-hewn walls were decorated with tapa cloth and an assortment of pagan objects—carved idols, feathered fetishes, calabashes made from coconut husks, notched war clubs, a pair of crossed spears with polished wood shafts and ivory barbs. Woven mats covered the floor; the furniture was of native lumber and bamboo. In one of the chairs a big man, young and ginger-haired, sat slumped on his spine with a glass propped on his chest. Judging from the bleary squint he directed at Quincannon, the glass contained *okolehao* or its equivalent and had been emptied and refilled several times.

"Who in blazes are you?" he demanded.

"My name is Quincannon."

"Quincannon? Scotsman, eh? I don't know any Scotsmen. Get out of my house."

"Not until I have what I came here for."

"And just what would that be?"

"Jack Vereen."

The name produced a twitch that nearly upset Millay's glass. "Don't know anybody by that name."

"No? You crossed the ocean from San Francisco with Vereen and his partner, Ben Joplin. Spent three nights carousing with them in Honolulu. Came here with Vereen yesterday."

"By Christ!" The exclamation startled the young Hawaiian girl, barefoot and dressed in a flowered sarong, who had just entered the room. "I don't want you any more, Mele," Millay snapped at her, and immediately she disappeared again. Then he said to Quincannon: "Casual companions, no more. What's your interest in them? Who the devil are you?"

Quincannon produced one of his business cards, laid it on the arm of Millay's chair. The rancher picked it up, squinted at it, and twitched again. He fortified himself with a deep draft from his glass before he said: "Detective? What's Vereen done to bring a detective all the way from San Francisco?"

"He's a notorious flim-flammer. His partner likewise. But then, I expect you know that by now."

"How would I know it? I had no business dealings with them."

"Where is Vereen now, Mister Millay?"

"No idea. In Hilo, I suppose. That's where I saw him last."

"The gent who runs the hotel in Kailua states otherwise," Quincannon said. "He contends Vereen was with you when you arrived two days ago."

"Bannister? The man is half blind and mostly senile. I was the only passenger to disembark at Kailua."

"If you're hiding Vereen on this ranch, you're guilty of aiding and abetting a fugitive."

"Hiding him? Why would I do that?"

"Why, indeed."

"Well, I'm not. Does he know you're after him?"

"If he doesn't, he soon will. I've come three thousand

miles to take him prisoner and I won't leave until I do."

"By God, search the house if you like. Search the entire ranch. You won't find a trace of the man because he was never here."

Quincannon said: "You haven't asked about his partner."

"What's that?"

"Vereen's partner. Ben Joplin, also known as the Nevada Kid. Where did you see him last? In their bungalow in Honolulu, mayhap?"

"No. I never went to their lodgings."

"Fortunate for you, if that's the truth. Joplin was shot to death there three nights ago."

In convulsive movements Millay drained his glass, slammed it down on a side table, and shoved onto his feet. "I don't know what you're talking about." The bluster was still in his voice, but it was underlain now by strong currents of fear. "And I've heard enough about matters that don't concern me. Either you rattle your hocks out of here, or I'll throw you out."

Quincannon's answer to that was a feral grin. In the tense moment that followed, there was the sudden pound of boots on the porch outside. Two pairs, one heavy, one light. A woman's voice called—"George? Are you in here?"—just before the screen door clattered open.

Quincannon moved a few paces to one side as the newcomers entered the room. The woman, in the lead, was an older, slimmer version of Millay—fair-skinned, her sun-bleached hair tucked inside a cowboy hat decorated by a flower *lei*. The hard-eyed man behind her was native-dark, bulky, dressed as she was in rough range garb. Grace Millay and Sam Opaka.

The woman glanced at Quincannon, said to her brother:

"Kolea told me we have company. Who is this man?"

"His name's Quincannon," Millay said. He seemed some calmer now that reinforcements had arrived, but no less defensive or truculent. "Detective from San Francisco. He thinks we're harboring one of the pair of swells I met on shipboard, supposed to be a confidence man."

"Lonesome Jack Vereen," Quincannon said.

"I told him I returned home alone yesterday. He doesn't believe me." To Quincannon he said: "This is my sister, Grace. And our foreman, Sam Opaka. Go ahead, ask them."

"He's telling the truth," Grace Millay said. Opaka said nothing, but his eyes, black and hard as volcanic rock, never left Quincannon's face. "There is no one on this ranch named Vereen. Nor has there ever been."

"Nor in Kailua, according to your brother," Quincannon said. "Abner Bannister tells a different tale."

Millay said: "I don't care what that old fool Bannister says. The last I saw of Jack Vereen was five minutes after the inter-island boat docked at Hilo. He was meeting someone there, he said."

"Did he, now? And who might that someone be?"

"He didn't confide in me. And I didn't ask. I keep my nose out of other men's business."

"You seem to have come a far distance for nothing, Mister Quincannon," Grace Millay said. "It appears your man is somewhere in Hilo."

"Perhaps. And perhaps not."

"Are you calling us liars?" Millay growled. He had picked up a decanter from the table and was about to re-plenish his glass. "All of us to our faces?"

His sister said warningly: "Be quiet, George."

"Why should I? I don't like anybody coming around here

206

making accusations, calling me a liar. I think we ought to kick his *okole* off our property. Sam and me, right now."

"I told you to be quiet. And put that decanter down. You've had enough to drink."

"The hell I have."

"More than enough." She nodded at Opaka. "Sam."

The *luna* moved for the first time. He caught hold of Millay's arm with one hand, the decanter with the other. He said softly—*"Pau."*—a word Quincannon had heard before and took to mean "enough, finished".

Millay started to argue, but when Opaka tightened his grip, the handsome features went lax and he subsided. He ran his tongue over dry lips, his gaze lowering, and meekly allowed Opaka to prod him from the room.

Grace Millay said: "Shall we go out on the *lanai*, Mister Quincannon? It's cooler there." And when they were outside in the shade of the monkey-pod: "You'll have to excuse my brother. He's . . . high-strung and inclined to be belligerent when he drinks too much."

Weak and easily manipulated were more apt descriptions. All fuss and feathers, with no sand; anyone who showed him strength, man or woman, could back him down. Prime prey for the likes of Vereen and the Nevada Kid. It was little wonder Millay chose to leave the ranch whenever he could, Quincannon thought. Only in the vice dens of Honolulu and San Francisco would he be able to convince himself that he was a man.

When he made no comment, she said: "This man you're looking for, Vereen . . . what sort of swindler is he?"

"The opportunistic sort. He and his partner suit their confidence games to the person or persons they're aiming to bilk. It isn't clear yet which one they tailored to your brother."

"*Were* they able to bilk him?"

"I can't say yet. You'll have to ask him."

"If they did, is the money recoverable?"

"That depends on how soon I catch Vereen. Any verifiable amount will be returned, of course."

"Of course." Her smile was thin and skeptical. She was a handsome woman, as Abner Bannister had said, but in a severe way. A woman hard rather than soft, cynical and tenacious, who would do whatever she felt necessary to protect her own. "You'll be leaving for Hilo, then?"

"Hilo, yes," he lied. "As soon as possible."

"The roads can be difficult to navigate in the dark. You may as well spend the night here . . . we have guest quarters out back. With an early start you'll reach Kailua in time to catch the afternoon steamer."

This suited Quincannon. He was tired and hungry, and a morning departure better fit his plans. He accepted the invitation. Grace Millay asked if he had luggage and said she would have it brought to him, and then summoned the Hawaiian girl, Mele, to show him to the guest house.

It was a large one-room affair, comfortably furnished. On the bedside table was a flat-wick lamp, of the kind that did not give off much light. A kerosene hanging lamp or lantern would produce a circle of flame and considerably more candlepower, but there was none of this type in the room. Where he would find one, he was sure, was in the stable.

Sam Opaka brought his carpetbag, handed it over, and departed without a word. Quincannon couldn't tell if the bag had been searched, not that it mattered a whit; it contained nothing of value or pertinence to his investigation. He washed away a layer of volcanic dust from his face, hands, and beard, and changed into fresh clothes for dinner.

The meal was served by lamplight on the porch or *lanai*. Home-grown beef, which he found surprisingly rich and tender, and a variety of Polynesian side dishes. He and Grace Millay were the only diners. George, she explained briefly, was not feeling well and preferred to remain in his room. As they ate, she questioned him again about his investigation, seeking details he was willing to provide—up to a point. He was candid about the exploits of Lonesome Jack Vereen and the Nevada Kid and his pursuit of the pair, but he kept the existence of the crude map and the *auohe* business to himself.

After dinner he declined the offer of brandy and returned to his quarters. He read from a volume of Walt Whitman's poetry for a time, with the Navy Colt on the bed beside him and one ear cocked. There was no incident of any kind, then or when he darkened the room and permitted himself two hours' sleep. An hour past midnight, he woke promptly, as he had trained himself to do, and slipped out of the guest house.

The night was silent, empty, the sky moonless and cloud-ridden. No lights showed in the ranch house; a dull lantern gleam in the bunkhouse was the only light to be seen. He crossed stealthily to the stable, let himself inside.

Stalled horses moved restlessly when he struck a lucifer. That one match was all he needed to find a lantern hanging from a nail near the door, take it down, and shake it to be sure its reservoir was mostly full. Wrapped in darkness again, he drifted out to where his hired wagon had been drawn near the corral fence and hid the lantern inside the box beneath the seat.

VII

Quincannon was up and on his way shortly after first light. The ranch had already stirred to life; *paniolos* and other hirelings moved among the buildings and in the yard. None of them paid any attention to him. He saw nothing of Sam Opaka, or of either of the Millays.

Roiling, dark-veined clouds obscured most of the towering slopes of Mauna Kea. They thickened and seemed to follow him, hiding the rising sun, as he clattered along the ranch road. Once he saw a lone rider far off among the cattle on an upper valley slope. Otherwise he had the road and the morning to himself.

When he came in sight of the sea, he spied more heavy clouds piling up on the horizon. The wind that rose and gusted here brought heat and humidity and the threat of another storm. But the threat had yet to be carried out by the time he reached the intersection with the Kailua road. He took this as a positive sign.

The road was deserted; he saw no one anywhere, heard only the thrum of the wind and the sullen mutter of the white-capped sea. He tethered the Kona Nightingale to the same stunted tree as yesterday, removed the lantern he had appropriated from under the seat. He considered donning the rain slicker that the wagon's owner had left rolled inside the box, but decided against it. Even if the storm broke while he was prowling among the rocks below, he would be better off unencumbered by an extra garment.

He made his way down to the ledge above the beach. The wind beat at him, stinging and wetting his face with spray from the breaking waves; the blowhole muttered and spouted, but its geysers were not as high flung as the ones yesterday. The broken outer walls of the *heiau* provided some shelter as he moved into the ruins. The first of the openings he'd discovered yesterday led him, after a dozen yards, into a cul-de-sac of broken, sharp-edged rock. The second wound deeper among the massive rocks, twisting enough so that he had to light the lantern in order to mark his progress, but it soon narrowed until he was unable to fit his body into the slit. Two more passages proved to be blocked and empty as well.

The fifth, at the far end of the arrangement of flat volcanic slabs, had a tight, half-hidden opening that required him to squeeze through sideways. After a short distance he could walk normally again. This was not a wholly natural passage, but one that had been widened and carved through the rock at a sharpening downward angle. Its floor had been worn smooth by water seepage; twice Quincannon slipped and nearly lost his balance. The walls were spotted with some kind of moss that crumbled when he brushed against it. The ceiling lowered as he went, so that he was forced to bow his body and move in an awkward waddle.

He had gone more than fifty rods, he judged, when the slant lessened and the passage ended in a cave-like opening that led into what must be an ancient tube. The seaward end was choked off by a jumbled wall of rock; the section that wound back inland appeared clear. Here it was cool and dry. The lantern's light glinted off a glass-smooth black floor, off streaks of color in the surrounding rock—earth minerals carried along by the lava flows and solidified among it.

After a short distance the tube grew clogged again, apparently with the residue of more recent flows, and at first he thought he'd stumbled into another cul-de-sac. Then, behind one of the boulders, he discovered a slender continuation of the tube. He had to crawl a ways on hands and knees, muttering to himself, all but nosing the lantern ahead of him like a kid engaged in a peanut-rolling contest, before it widened again. Now hanging stalactites and jutting stalagtites obstructed his progress; one of the former gouged his neck in passing and earned itself a colorful name. The tunnel narrowed, curved, rose slightly, then once more widened, this time to merge with another, larger tube.

No sooner had he entered this one than a faint current of warm, fresh air tickled his nostrils.

So. The tube must have another entrance, or at the least an outside vent, somewhere ahead. He quickened his pace, walking upright now, holding the lantern high. The floor here bore small cracks and the footing was more certain. Ahead, the tube widened and piles of round, smooth stones lined one of the walls. They seemed to have been arranged by primitive hands into a pattern—the first indication of human habitation. The fresh-air current was stronger; he had a briny whiff of the sea.

Around another turning, he found the *auohe*.

And something else he had not expected to find.

This section of the tube was some twenty feet in width, its stalactitic ceiling pressed low, as if spread by great force from above. The floor and the lower parts of the walls were grayish black, here and there streaked with encrustations of green and rusty red. Above and ahead, more recent lava flows had formed an embankment of solid glistening black that rose, with another upslope of the ceiling, into a jagged ledge some fifteen feet above. The air here was no longer quite so fresh. The odor that assaulted Quincannon's nostrils was that of mold and rot.

Part of the embankment had been carved into a terrace of shelves. On these lay dozens of skeletons, some wrapped in decaying tapa cloth, others arranged on powdery mats, one wearing an elaborate necklace made of shark's or whale's teeth fastened with braided hair. Piles of bones and detached skulls were heaped together in hewn niches. Interspersed among these grisly remains were artifacts of the sort he had seen in the Millay ranch house—fiber nets, drums covered with some sort of fish or animal skin, rotting feather standards, spears and arrows and daggers, calabashes and gourds and woven baskets.

But it was none of this that triggered his sudden wrath. He subscribed to the theory espoused by Mark Twain's Pudd'nhead Wilson: When angry, count to four; when very angry, swear. And so he blued the air with a string of sulphurous oaths the originality of which would have made Mr. Clemens himself proud.

For he stood not just in an ancient burial cave, but in a modern one as well. The human remains that lay sprawled at the base of the embankment was a long way yet from being a skeleton. And even at a distance, the upturned face was identifiable in the flickery lantern light.

He had finally caught up with Lonesome Jack Vereen.

A quick inspection of the corpse revealed two bullet wounds, one in the upper body and the other to the left temple. The same fate as his partner, but not by Vereen's hand this time—if, in fact, it had been his hand that had done for the Nevada Kid. Quincannon set the lantern down and searched Vereen's pockets. His client's stock certificates were not there. Nor was so much as a single coin or greenback, much less R. W. Anderson's missing $5,000.

He bit off another long-jointed oath, lifted the lantern again, and stood up. He swung the light along the shelves for a closer inspection of the artifacts scattered among the bones. None of them seemed to be of particular worth ex-

cept to an archeologist or a museum curator. So then what
was it about the burial cave that had fired the blood of
scalawags like Vereen and the Nevada Kid? Had something
else been buried here at one time, something that was now
in the Millays' possession?

Pondering, Quincannon turned away from the open
crypts. In the sweep of light as he did so, his eye caught
movement among the rocks on the high ledge farther down.
His reaction was immediate, instinctive, and life saving.

He already had flung himself sideways when the rifle
flash came.

VIII

The lantern burst from his hand and went crashing and
clattering across the floor. He landed on his right shoulder
and skidded into the opposite wall, the boom of the shot repeated in a dozen lusty reverberating echoes all around him.
Two seconds later the Navy Colt was in his hand and he
was lying flat with the weapon held out in front of him.

There was another shot, the slug missing high and show-
ering him with lava chips and dust. Behind him, the shattered lantern had left a trail of burning kerosene, but the
reservoir by now must have been a quarter or less full; the
flames were low and before the sniper on the ledge could
trigger a third shot, they flickered out. The tube was
plunged into blackness as thick as tar.

Quincannon scrambled backward and sideways toward
the middle of the cave. Then he froze in place. The stillness
that followed was as absolute as the dark. Now he and whoever had been trying to kill him were on equal footing; if either fired, the barrel flash would betray his position and

make him a clear target.

A stalemate, but one that couldn't last. Sooner or later one of them would have to make a move.

Minutes crept away, how many he had no idea. In such darkness you quickly lost track of time. And it was difficult, if not impossible, to gauge the exact source of any sounds—both an advantage and a disadvantage. Notions formed in Quincannon's head. He discarded all but one.

His heightened sense of smell picked up a new scent on the air currents. And then something broke the silence—a distant dripping and thrumming. Ozone. Wind and rain. The Kona storm had commenced outside. Before the ambush, he would have grumbled at the fact. Now he saw it as a potential boon to his chances.

The second entrance must be somewhere up near the ledge where the shooter was hidden, so the sounds of the storm would be louder in his ears. That would make any noises down here even harder to pinpoint. In his mind's eye Quincannon could see the shape of the burial chamber here and his relative position. He calculated the distance to the turning behind him. And then he moved, propelling himself backward and sideways on forearms and knees, deliberately making as much clatter as he could.

As expected, he drew no fire. He skittered across to the embankment, then backward into the turning. The floor there was not as smooth; sharp edges ripped through his clothing, gouged and sliced into his skin. He permitted himself a small outcry at one of the sharper cuts of pain. When his hands or feet encountered loose rock, he sent them rattling across the floor. Still he drew no fire. The confusion of sounds were his ally, and so was the fact that the farther he withdrew along the tube, the more the sounds would diminish in the rifleman's ears. That was the one thing that could be marked in utter darkness—the fading of sounds that told of attempted escape back the way he'd come.

Once he was into the turning, he clawed himself upright and felt his way backward along the wall, still generating random sounds. He kept this up until he reached the juncture with the first tube and entered that one. He'd gone far enough by then, he judged, to have passed out of earshot. He stood still, waiting, listening to silence.

It might have been five minutes or ten or fifteen that he stood there. He was a man of steel nerves, but the pitch black had begun to have a faintly claustrophobic effect on him. The urge to strike a lucifer was strong. Instead, he made his way back into the larger tube and began to pick his way along the wall, stealthily this time, pausing and straining to hear after every other step. The silence remained so acute it was like a pressure against his eardrums.

When he finally arrived at the turning into the burial cave, he stepped out from the wall and took the packet of lucifers from his pocket. He set himself and snicked one alight on his thumbnail, then immediately snuffed the flame and flung himself to one side.

Nothing happened. There was no shot.

He changed position and struck three more matches before he was satisfied that his trick had worked. The rifleman had believed that he sought escape through the ruins, had likely gone down to the *heiau* to set up another ambush there.

With another lucifer held aloft, Quincannon made his way to where the ledge jutted overhead. Two more matches showed him the way up to it, and then the opening that led out of the tube. This passage, like the one in the temple, had been hand-hewn through porous rock and proved to be a much easier and more direct route to and from the burial chamber. It wound and twisted narrowly, climbed, dipped for fifty yards or so. The currents of air grew stronger, the beat of rain and distant thunder louder. One last rise, and then he could see a slit of wet, gray daylight ahead.

He approached the aperture cautiously, his Navy cocked and ready. Outside, he could make out a small flat space surrounded by glistening black rock. He eased his head through the opening. Rain fell in a silvery curtain, but the full force of the storm had yet to be unleashed; the sky was the color of a livid purple and black bruise. The hiss and pound of the running seas was like a low cannonade. But all he could see was rock. He stepped out, hunted up a declivity that led out of the flat space, followed it until he reached a point where the ocean came into view. A few seconds after that, there was a loud boom and a spout of water burst upward below and to his left—the blowhole erupting again.

Now he knew where he was. The path down from the road, he judged, should be close by. This proved to be the case. He found it, hunkered there to reconnoiter. The ledge and the blowhole were now visible, but there was no sign of the shooter. Mindful of the slick footing, he started down.

He had almost reached the ledge before he spied his adversary, forted up behind a rock with the barrel of his rifle trained on the entrance to the *heiau*. The man's identity came as no surprise—Sam Opaka, the Millays' *luna*. Sent to do George Millay's bidding, or possibly his sister's. Quincannon paused to wipe a sheen of rain and spray from his eyes before he closed the distance between himself and the Hawaiian.

His foot dislodged a stone, sent it rattling down. It was a small noise, all but lost in the voices of storm and sea, but somehow Opaka must have heard it. Either that, or the man possessed a sixth sense for danger. He moved with a suddenness that surprised Quincannon, in one motion levering himself to his feet and bringing the rifle to bear. He fired first, by a fraction of a second; the bullet ricocheted harmlessly off rock. Quincannon's shot, even though hurried and off aim, found Opaka's arm or shoulder and caused him to lose his grip on the rifle. But it didn't take him down. He shouted something, a sound even wilder than the storm, and charged as Quincannon reached the ledge.

It was not in Quincannon's nature to shoot an unarmed man. Then again, it was not in his nature to lose either a skirmish or his life by standing on principle. He triggered a round at the onrushing man. And to his astonishment, he missed—an exceedingly rare occurrence that he later blamed on the storm and the poor footing. He had no chance to fire a third time. Opaka crashed into him and sent them both tumbling across the fissured surface of the ledge.

The blowhole fountained with a roar just then, drenching them both with its downpour. They rolled over in a clinch, Opaka coming up on top as foamy water swirled and tugged around them. But he was one-armed now; the bullet must have shattered bone in the other and rendered it useless. Even so, he was bull-strong and fending him off was no easy task. A thump to the side of the head rattled Quincannon's brains and made him very angry. He swore, bucked, and heaved the *luna* off him. The Navy was still in his hand; he cracked Opaka on the cheek with the barrel, a blow that sent him reeling.

When the Hawaiian staggered upright, he was close to the blowhole. In the tube below, the surf snarled and hissed and let loose another jet of water. The boil of it coming out of the mouth-like opening churned up around Opaka's feet, caused him to lose his balance. He fell, sliding and splashing in the backflow, clawing at the rock as he was pulled backward.

There was nothing Quincannon could do. An instant later, in a wild churning of arms and legs, Sam Opaka vanished into the blowhole.

IX

The storm had blown through by the time Quincannon reached the Millay Ranch. Small comfort—he was bedraggled and soaked to the skin. And still furious.

He found Grace Millay in the stable, helping one of the *paniolos* tend to a foundered horse. She showed little emotion while he told her what had happened in the lava tube and what he had found there, but the news of Sam Opaka's death struck her like a blow. She wavered, steadied herself against the stable wall with her eyes squeezed shut. It took half a minute for her to regain her equilibrium. When she opened her eyes again, it was as if she had never lost control at all.

"I didn't send him after you," she said.

"But you did know about the burial cave."

"George and I found it when we were children. I'm not proud of this, but, after my father died, we brought some of the artifacts up here to the house."

"Objects of value?"

"Hardly. It's the burial place of the high priest who ordered the *heiau* built, his and his family's." A vein throbbed in her forehead; the cords in her neck stood out in sharp relief. "It's still *kapu*. Sam Opaka was a half-caste, but he held to the old beliefs. He wouldn't have violated the taboo on his own initiative."

"But he would have on orders from your brother."

"My brother." She said it bitterly, with a measure of disgust. "Yes, he would have. Sam was fiercely loyal to both of us."

"Loyal enough to commit mayhem evidently."

"I don't believe he was trying to kill you. And I don't believe he killed that swindler Vereen. Neither Sam nor I ever laid eyes on the man, nor knew anything about him until you came."

Quincannon said: "We'll go have a talk with your brother now."

George Millay was in his study in the ranch house, working over a set of ledgers. He looked up as they entered, started at the sight of Quincannon. His handsome face was pale and drawn in the lamplight, blood-veined eyes bearing further witness to the hangover he was suffering.

His sister went straight to the desk. "Stand up," she commanded.

"Grace. . . ."

"Stand up, I said."

He lifted himself slowly out of his chair, and, when he was upright, she fetched him a roundhouse slap. It had the force of a whip crack, staggering him. "Sam is dead," she said. "Do you hear me? Sam . . . is . . . dead!"

Millay blinked several times, fingering his cheek, before her words registered. "Sam? Oh, God, what . . . ?" His bloodshot eyes focused on Quincannon. "You!" he said to Quincannon. "You were in the *heiau*. You killed him."

"I believed he was trying to kill me. On your orders."

"No! I didn't tell him to do that. Only scare you off if. . . ."

"If I found the burial chamber. And what you left there."

Millay made a faint moaning sound. He sat down again, heavily, and held his head in his hands. His voice, when it came, was low and thick with pity for himself. "That bastard Vereen gave me no choice. It was self-defense. He had a pistol, he forced me to take him into the cave. He would've shot me when he saw there really wasn't any cloak. Almost did. If he hadn't stumbled. . . ."

"Cloak?"

"Feather cloak. Damn non-existent feather cloak."

His sister said: "You fool, you buffoon. You told him *that?*"

"I was trying to impress a woman in San Francisco . . . I didn't see any harm in making the claim that far from home. Vereen and Joplin were there at the time, within earshot. They booked passage on the same ship, struck up an acquaintance . . . pretended to be businessmen, sports. I didn't find out they were crooks until the last night in Honolulu."

Quincannon produced the crude map. "Who drew this?"

"I did. Joplin asked for it."

"When Vereen wasn't present, no doubt. Double-crossers, the pair of them. What happened that last night? You went with them to their bungalow on Hoapili Street, eh?"

"Vereen's idea. Discuss a business proposition . . . they wanted me to let them broker the cloak to a rich man they knew in Los Angeles. I tried to tell them then that I'd made up the story, but they wouldn't believe me. Kept feeding me *okolehao* and I . . . I must've passed out."

"And when you came to, Joplin was dead and Vereen claimed you'd shot him."

Millay nodded. The motion made him wince. There was

a decanter of clear liquid on the desk; he reached for it. Grace snatched it away from him.

"Grace, please. . . ."

"No. You've had enough of this poison."

"I killed two men, Grace. Three, if Sam's dead. There's not enough *okolehao* in the world to make me forget that."

Quincannon said: "Like as not, you didn't kill Ben Joplin. My guess is Vereen murdered his partner and blamed you to gain a hold over you. And to take this feather cloak, whatever it is, for himself."

"Two or three, what's the difference?" Then: "I tried again to tell Vereen there wasn't any cloak. He wouldn't listen. Threatened to turn me in to police if I didn't take him to the burial cave."

"And after you managed to shoot him dead, you emptied his pockets."

"I was afraid to leave anything that might identify him if the body were ever found."

"What did you do with what you took? And with his luggage? If you tell me you disposed of it all into the sea, I promise you'll be the one sorry lad."

"No. I threw the luggage away, kept the money and some stock certificates."

"Ah. Let's have the lot."

Millay had hidden the items in his desk. R. W. Anderson's missing stocks were all there, but the amount of cash was considerably less than $5,000. The rest must have been spent by the thieves; Millay swore the handful of bills was all he'd taken from Vereen.

Quincannon counted them carefully. The total amount was $1,120. He said: "You will arrange for a bank draft, payable to John Quincannon, in the amount of three thousand eight hundred and eighty dollars."

Grace Millay asked: "Why should we do that?"

He told her why.

"And then what? What do you plan to do about the two dead men?"

Mollified now, Quincannon said: "Nothing, as long as the draft is honored at your Honolulu bank. Your brother claims the shooting was self-defense . . . I have no reason to doubt the veracity of that, and no jurisdiction in such matters in any case. As for Vereen's remains, if the bones of ancient priests have no objection to those of a murdering grifter's lying among them, I have none either."

He left the Millay Ranch for the last time a short while later, with the stock certificates and a signed letter authorizing the bank draft tucked into the pocket of a dry coat, and with the answer to a final question supplied by Grace Millay. The feather cloak which had precipitated all the trouble was in fact a priceless garment made for Hawaiian kings from the tiny, delicate yellow feathers of now extinct Oo and Mamo birds. Kamehameha's cloak, one of the few known to exist and which now reposed in the Bishop Museum in Honolulu, contained hundreds of thousands of these feathers and reputedly had taken several women fifty years to finish. Feather cloaks were not made for high priests; there had never been any such treasure in the burial cave on Millay land.

Such was the stuff of lies, deceit, greed, and murder.

X

Two days later Quincannon was back in Honolulu. But he didn't stay on there as he had planned to do at the beginning of his manhunt. Once he had the full $5,000 safely in hand, he booked passage on the next ship bound for San Francisco. The various pleasures to be found in the Nuuanu Avenue Port of Hell district no longer appealed to him. His misadventures on the Big Island were partly responsible, but the primary reason was that he missed San Francisco in general and Sabina in particular. Dear Sabina, not only his capable partner but the love of his life. Even if his passion was thus far unrequited and she stubbornly refused to succumb to ploys, manipulations, entreaties, or any other method of honest seduction. Perhaps the shell brooch he had picked out for her in a Merchant Street shop would make her more receptive. Not that that was the reason he'd bought the present, of course. His motives, as always where she was concerned, were pure.

When the ship sailed out of Honolulu harbor, he stood at the rail for his last glimpse of Hawaii's tropical lushness. Now that he was leaving, his feelings toward the islands had mellowed. They had their allure, to be sure. At another time, under different circumstances, he might have actually found them stimulating.

The mellowness lasted until the ship was three hours out from Oahu. That was when yet another tropical storm put in a sudden appearance and set the sea achurn, the steamer rolling, and Quincannon lurching to his stateroom.

He lay in bed, green-gilled and groaning, and vowed that he would shoot himself before he took another ocean voyage. As for paradise, he thought morosely, one man's version was another man's aversion. Like beauty, it was all in the eye—and the stomach—of the beholder.